Whispers
in the Cries

Matthew Ewald

BLACK BED
SHEET

Whispers in the Cries
A Black Bed Sheet/Diverse Media Book
December 2011

Library of Congress Control Number: 2011944591

ISBN-10: 0-9833773-6-7
ISBN-13: 978-0-9833773-6-8

Whispers in the Cries

A Black Bed Sheet/Diverse Media Book
Antelope, CA

ACKNOWLEDGEMENTS

This, now more than ever,
is for my parents.

May we always find
one another...

Even if only
"for a little while."

~~~~~~~~~

For my mentor and pal, Wayne. Thank you
for the guidance, thank you for the knowledge
and support, and thank you for braving the
darkness of this horror beside me.

~~~~~~~~~

And for the one I've come to call *"Old Salt."*
Whoever you were, whoever you are
~~ may our paths cross again...

In this life or the next.

Whispers in the Cries

Matthew Ewald

"*I did not tell half of what I saw, for I knew I would not be believed...*"

⸺ Marco Polo
(On his deathbed, *1324.*)

PROLOGUE:
HAUNTED

*"There are demon-haunted worlds,
regions of utter darkness."*

-- The Isa Upanishad
(India, ca. 600 B.C.)

•

"The time will come..."

The words slid into the man's consciousness like a hissing radiator.

"...when, with elation, you will greet yourself arriving at your own door, in your own mirror, and each will smile at the other's welcome--

He looked at himself in the dirty mirror, looking at his reflection. Hand on his forehead, fingers disappearing into sweat-slicked hair. Glistening from desperation, eyes like bullet holes staring back at him. Eyes that had seen too much.

Veins pulsing in his temples, reddish-pink worms. The beats in rhythm with his heart. He had lost everything.

--and say, sit here. Eat. You will love again the stranger who was your self--

He turned to look at his profile, the left side. He wanted to face the wall, not the window. The wall was empty. The window was life on the outside. Head dropping like an anvil, he watched his nostrils flare, each hand gripping the edge of the counter-top, spattered with stains ignored for the better part of three days.

Nothing. He felt a void, but for the pain that was so consuming that each tear that now fell seemed to etch scars into his cheeks.

--Give wine. Give bread. Give back your heart to itself, to the stranger who has loved you all your life, whom you ignored for another, who knows you by heart--

He looked past the stains--dried water droplets, breakfast grease--at the reflections on the grey surface. His hands trembled, muscle and sinew taut from shoulder to wrist. Spilling into the sink just inches away, more than half a dozen bottles with familiar prescription labels in white and yellow. Anti-depressants, pills of every color for schizophrenia. A color for every voice.

From Zoloft to Celexa, Abilify to Zyprexa. Increases in dosage, little stragglers of pills, ones that were no longer effective. And the big green bottle of Excedrin Migraine.

Looking toward the wall again, not the window and the nighttime neon and the happiness of everyone else in this damnable city, his eyes fell onto the brightly polished gun. A military issue 1911 Colt .45. The magazine was out and one round upright and tall beside it. Both items polished proudly; catching the light that hung from the kitchen ceiling, a small room really. Nothing more than the counter top, that dirty mirror, a sink and a refrigerator that had scratches on it, white on the yellowed surface. Layers.

Knowing what that cold steel would soon taste. Was that the gun talking to him? Or the face in the mirror?

--take down the love letters from the bookshelf, the photographs, the desperate notes--

A photograph was clipped to the mirror's edge, slipped into the frame at an angle. Still, the corners were long ago dog-eared and cracked, discolored by age. Pictured was a handsome young man and a beautiful woman, smaller and younger--did it really matter to describe them? He already knew, had known for so long...they were sharing a kiss that would forever be felt upon his lips. An embrace that seemed a lifetime ago.

An echo of love and loss.

--peel your own image from the mirror."

The man studied himself in that mirror, putting the photograph out of his mind, his eyes going wide and alert. Aware. Something was coming...

Laughter from the darkness of the hall past his left shoulder. Then...children singing. A pool of tentacles sliding over the cheap tile at the entrance to the room. A devil's grin in the darkness, away from the counter, away from the window.

"Sit."

The open bathroom door slammed shut, the pill bottles bounced in the sink.

"Feast on your life."

The young man smiled, understanding completely as he lifted the Colt.

BANG.

PART ONE:
HOMECOMING

"Our life is made by the death of others."

-- Leonardo Da Vinci, 1452-1519.

"So we keep asking, over and over,
Until a handful of earth
Stops our mouths --
But is that an answer?"

-- Heinrich Heine,
Lazarus (1854)

CHAPTER ONE

Grillo's Gym
October 22, 2011, 2:15 PM.

Blood and sweat mingled on Randy Conroy's temple. A solid hit just above his left eye from the larger man weaving and dodging in front of him. To any bystander, it was a blur of dragon tattoos from one and the smooth yet brutal moves of another who had clearly studied the martial arts. And because of it, Conroy was able to keep a complete focus on his sparring partner.

A few droplets of blood meant nothing to him, a small cut from his last tussle had re-opened, big-fucking-deal. He knew there were spectators--the blonde with the grey sweat pants on the Stairmaster a dozen feet away being a good example--staring at his chiseled jaw, his piercing eyes. A small bump on his nose that could only be seen in profile.

Conroy had more concentration by pure willpower than in any technique his larger opponent could garner from his own trained skills. Outside of Grillo's, he might be seen with a slight swagger as he walked past the storefronts along Desmond Avenue, checking out the women sipping drinks outside of Sluggers, while their boyfriends watched the big screen hi-defs above the bar. He'd nod, often getting an acknowledgment.

The girls never noticing that Conroy looked much younger than his true years.

1

Here, it was a different story altogether, in the ring he was like a pilot aiming for the runway on the smallest runway in the southern US. Grillo allowed paying customers to bring in a guest once a month, and so at times a group of four workout buddies became eight. Those who were not "local," or familiar to the neighborhood or the set-up of the well-lit place in general, might question the veracity of a college-age "kid" going toe-to-toe with a downright frightening looking man, with the muscles of someone who had done serious time.

But Conroy liked to pick his battles. He *liked* this battle. He squeezed his eye shut to get the stream of blood to mingle in his eyebrow and leave his vision clear. Fit, toned, this summer he felt his own personal best when it came to peak physical perfection, but tonight...he was losing.

Badly.

He was doing his best, keeping it up. Overhead lights showing every little detail of his opponent's face, the gap between two of his lower teeth. Conroy knew his own face looked worse, just that one small cut, but the fatigue was there. He was keeping up, giving it the good fight. Landing a few punches in between taking a couple of good hits. He kept at it though.

Kept on coming. Started to wear the other guy down.

Grillo's Gym wasn't upscale, sunlight streamed through yellowed blinds--stained by cigarette smoke in the decades before the new ordinances--but it also wasn't a rundown pit for guys on their way out, trying for one last dream comeback that would never happen.

See, Jimmy Grillo wasn't what you'd call a Donald Trump, but he had seen the writing on those nicotine-stained walls a half-dozen years ago. Buildings being torn down up the main stem, condos filling the vacant lots. The gym was no longer exclusive for training boxers, with floors filled with saliva from discarded mouth guards.

His family had owned the building since the 1950s, and now he was the only Grillo left. And the building, while indiscreet, was two stories high and was a corner lot. And so the building effectively had two addresses, 39 South Wallace, which had the neon sign with the boxing gloves bip bapping, and down a more darkened street, was his joint. The way it had been for decades. But he had torn out part of the ground floor, hung up some motivational posters and–voila!–115 East Desmond was now the entrance to New Decade Fitness.

People bought into titles. And so one wall was lined with young women in their tight bodies all the way to the old gals trying to drop the pounds and cellulite before their fortieth class reunion. Young and old, doesn't matter. And the second floor was a dream. For those into vanity, not into trying to stay trim.

Grillo had taken out a loan and put in a few treadmills and moved the existing weight benches around. All so men like Dragon Biceps could grunt in the window, the sports bar with its bored women directly across the street. Grillo had paid that initial loan off within a year.

Grillo *was* like Trump in one way, he knew assets when he saw them. And fitness was an asset. But he prided himself in not having an entire wall

3

lined with the bright colors of vending machines hawking protein drinks, so-called vitamin enriched water, and the newest fad: Muscle Milk, its white bottle with the logo of the local sports team set to optimum visibility.

He did sell Gatorade, though. The original and the orange-flavored, because women seemed to like it more. And he still sold the sixteen ounce bottles a little over cost. It was a place where you worked hard and played hard. And, yes, checked out the parade of flesh, but not be encumbered by the sight of personal trainers that were built like swamp monsters.

Male *and* female.

As Randy started into an arc that would hopefully land a solid hit on Dragon Tattoos' face for the first time in two minutes, he saw Grillo come out of his office, a small rectangle of red brick, big brawl posters visible through a spotless window. Sonny Liston. Cassius Clay.

"Yo, Randy!"

The boxing glove connected, brief exaltation at the expulsion of air from his opponent's mouth.

"Randy!" Louder. Grillo moving forward like a steam shovel.

"Hey, Jimmy. What's up?" Fists up, a truce. No dirty fighting.

"Telephone."

"Can't you see that I'm a little busy here, Jimmy?" Laughing with a tinge of annoyance. Grillo usually just took messages. He started to make his signature stance.

"Randy--"

"Come on, man. Really?" Gloves in the air, not a truce, now in exasperation. He leaned in to the other guy before turning away toward Grillo. "*I'll have you down on the mat in a minute, you're losing it now.*"

"Phone call for you, pal. Some guy calling from back home."

"Yeah...and?" He dropped his fists back down, nodded, and the pummeling started anew. Two seconds later, he's plowed by a nasty right hook. Stumbles back against the ropes.

Grillo had been moving with determination the whole time. His white-knuckled hands, scarred going back to when Randy was in grade school, were balled into fists. He dragged his substantial girth toward Randy, laid a meaty hand on the younger man's shoulder. Slick with sweat.

"You can take it in my office. It's family, kid."

Randy didn't even offer him a look of indifference.

"Look, Randy." Grillo had known Randy a long time, he hated to have to just spit this out on his own. "I'm sorry," he tightened his grip on his young protégé's shoulder, pulling him away into his corner hard. "Your grandpa passed away, kid."

Randy turned and looked at him hard. And then...then he shrugged.

"Take a message."

Then he turned, and the match resumed. Before Grillo had a chance to shut the door to his office, Randy charged in and scored a K.O. for the first time in over a year.

For the first time in a long time, he finally felt...alive.

5

CHAPTER TWO

Locker Room. 3:50 PM.

Grillo entered the locker room as Randy deftly unwrapped his taped-up hands.

"I love ya like a son," the beefy man said, "but don't ever put me in that kind of position again."

"And what position is that, Jimmy-boy?"

"Your mother is fuckin' scary, kid."

"Yeah," Randy tossed the bandages onto the bench. "She is a real piece of work...Hey, let me talk with you after I get my shower, all right."

"Sure thing," Grillo said, tapping the locker nearest his slab-of-meat hand. They walked in opposite directions.

Ten minutes later—during Randy's upbringing, he took what both his father and grandfather referred to as "Army showers"--he was walking past the lockers toward the metal door that had creaked since before he was born. Same with the EXIT sign and how it fizzled, no doubt.

Pink-faced, hair still wet, he knocked on Grillo's door before walking in.

The other office, this one hidden away in the men's locker room that instantly stung at your nostrils upon entering with the salty tang of ancient sweat, was just as run-down as its owner. The main office out front was for show, for the tight bodied women in the expensive sports bras and fresh coat of make-up. *This* office, the one Randy now stood in, was where the rats went to die.

"I'm sorry about your grandpa," Grillo had his size twelve shoes propped on a battered desk covered with coffee-stained newspapers. He paused for a second. "When are you heading back?"

"Back?" Randy looked at Grillo in a confused way.

"Family feuds or not, he's your grandfather, kid."

"*Was my grandfather*, past tense." He looked at a poster on the wall, then back at Grillo. "Hell, he probably had a heart attack just remembering our last conversation."

"That was between you and your parents, you told me so. The old man wasn't a part of that."

"Yeah, well he was there," Randy said, ruefully. His blue eyes widened with fading impatience, as if by focusing his glare he might lower his heart rate. Two dull spots now, the color of blood diamonds.

"And opinions vary." Grillo matched his stare, teacher to apt pupil. "You should go back."

"And take care of my *business*. Right, Jimmy?" Laughing and sighing at the same time, a deflated balloon in the dank locker room office. His response almost orchestrated with a trademarked dryness of humor. Those who knew him well, and not just in passing, knew that he was quite the talented actor.

Grillo knew this, and he wasn't even part of the live studio audience.

"Take care of your *family*." Leaning in on that last word, the important one. "They still are, you know. Your *family*." Hammering the word in.

7

Randy ran his hands on either side of his hair, pulling the long strands behind his ears. Droplets of water touched his shirt collar.

"Why are you even pushing this? It has nothing to do with you." He really didn't care himself. "I mean...what? What do you think is going to happen? That I'll suddenly appear at my parents' doorstep and they'll run to me with tears in their eyes, applause filling the room?"

He looked down at the tiled floor. Someone had used a pen knife on it to commemorate New Year's Eve, 1982.

"It just doesn't work like that."

Randy was out the door and back in the locker room before the sentence was even finished. Jimmy on his heels, a massive stride. A worn-down titan giving pursuit.

Randy scooped up his wrapping tape off of the bench, one stretch still bloody from his K.O., and threw it into his locker. His head felt stiff. He didn't care, he just wanted out. But there was no getting rid of blood on blood.

"Just...go away, Jimmy. We're not in the ring, I don't need a coach."

Grillo understood completely. He could shut his eyes and hear the tick-tick-ticking of a time bomb with the fuse running low. Yeah, the apt pupil and the teacher.

"I'm not your father, and I *know* I'm not your blood," he kept at Randy, keeping his own tick-ticking in check. "But I became responsible for you the minute...no, the *second* you walked in that door, and I'm getting tired of the sound of your disrespectful gums flappin'."

Grillo's hand went from finger-stabbing the locker room door to pointing at the floor.

"The least you could do is show me some goddamn respect in my own gym."

Randy went silent, humbled.

"Look, Jimmy. I'm--"

"Naw, I get it. You're a big hotshot journalist at a struggling newspaper, the thing would go under if it wasn't for your articles. You're worried about job security, worried about all those materialistic items all you young people care so much for these days. Just like those women on the Stairmasters with sweat running down their spines."

Grillo was on a roll now.

"All your technology and your toys. Even your looks are a status symbol. But let me tell you, when I was your age, I never had some kind of workout music playing in my head. Now this thing with your grandpa...you take it out on me. That's all well and good, better me than you. Because I keep seeing you mad at the world, blaming everybody."

He lowered his tone.

"Self-doubt is a powerful drug, but the past is the past, kid. I don't get why you constantly beat yourself up over it."

"I don't know," Randy was still sullen. "Maybe because my mother's not here to do it for me." Then he fell silent.

Grillo turned slowly, not speaking. When his back was fully turned, he thought that the kid had too many hard hits, just another sob story. He was stretching himself thin, working his ass off at the paper and then coming here to sweat all the frustrations out.

9

"We're all livin' on borrowed time, Randy." Grillo shot back from over his shoulder. "The only thing that's left of the past are memories and the ghosts that haunt them."

He stopped in front of one of the Fight Night posters, a large promotional in stark black and white turned to fading sepia. His own face, back when the nose was only broken once, and recently at that. It had been an undercard fight, yet it was one of the few times that he had ever felt truly alive.

The cracks of age distorted his features now, betraying nothing but his eyes. And those sang out a different tale, ringing like the bell that ended each round on the mat. *You want to hear a sob story? Get in line.*

"Life is just too damn short kid," he said, feeling like he was repeating himself….and perhaps he was, only this time he wasn't chiding himself. "Pretty soon there's nothing left of us. Just dust and echoes… Dust and echoes." The last came out in a whisper.

His meaty hand reached for the door.

"Words of advice, one last time. Go home, make amends before it's too late."

And then the door swung closed, a dull echo followed. Blood and sweat still hanging thick in the air. Randy slammed his locker door hard enough that, if Grillo had still been there, his teeth would have rattled in his skull.

Too late?

"Already is..." Not knowing if he was saying it out loud, or not.

CHAPTER THREE

October 24, 2011, Mound, Minnesota.

They'd actually held the viewing at D'elaqua Funeral Home an extra day so that Randy could be allowed his proper respects. American Airlines Flight 1983 to Minneapolis, followed by an hour's drive west. Randy had hoped that his "delayed arrival" would save him from this...this *nightmare*.

The middle of Minnesota, and yet the strains of Lynyrd Skynyrd's "Sweet Home Alabama" rang true, a favorite on every tavern jukebox. Randy had the heater pumped to the max in his rented Toyota the entire ride. Not yet Halloween, yet the leaves had long since brightened, died, and were in the process of falling into the ditches. At times, the wind outside picked up to a howl, but Randy knew that it was from the open, empty expanse, and nothing more.

And if that wasn't enough, a storm rolled in from the Dakotas just as the funeral was winding down. A hard rain, dark clouds spilling out their bellies. He was hardened by the rapid change in weather, he had grown up here. And back in Manhattan, the tall buildings made the winds shriek just as loud.

Later, at the cemetery, one of the funeral attendants came up to stand beside him before the closed casket. A blue tent covered the crowd, but the rain still hit those at the edge.

"Did you know him well?"

Randy was momentarily startled, but quickly kept his surprise in check. *Always the fighter*.

"He was my grandfather." Thinking, goes to show that even his relatives didn't recognize him anymore, if some of them ever did.

"Doesn't answer my question." The old man pressed on. He was dressed in a black suit far more expensive than anything Randy himself had owned. Or cared to own. His family was all about material things. Couple of dozen people standing in groups, stoic, like displays of mannequins in Bloomingdales back home. His *true* home.

The man leaned back and Randy saw another man of equal age looking over at him, one eyebrow raised. Not acknowledging Randy by name, either. Yet, truth be told, Randy didn't remember half the names of those gathered.

The one next to him retrieved a flask from his inside jacket pocket and downed a quick gulp of courage. At least, that was the phrase in the bistros back in SoHo. For this guy, it might have been a quick remedy for the shakes.

And not the arthritic kind.

He didn't look at Randy when he continued.

"Doesn't really matter, you think you know someone, then they end up in a fucking asylum painting pretty pictures with crayons in a padded cell." He paused, as if wanting to continue. Rain pelted the tent like a heartbeat.

"Excuse me?" Randy looked at him, hard. Yet the man didn't turn.

"Pfft."

"What did you say?" His voice like steel, his eyes narrowing as if he were facing Dragon Tattoos and not some pretentious old bastard.

"Well, what do ya know, ain't that cute," the liquor making the relative run off on one long sentence. "Oh, yeah, grandson doesn't know about dear old granddad's deep, dark secrets." Followed by drunken laughter in a foggy haze of what was no doubt top shelf booze.

He gave a rebuttal and put a chubby arm around Randy.

"Or should I say...the *family's* deep, dark secrets." Looking Randy in the eye for the first time.

At this point, Randy was genuinely confused, standing there and studying the drunk before him.

"Good for you for getting out," the man said around another quick slurp. "Escaping."

Pointing a finger at Randy to enunciate what he thought to be a grand word, an important word.

"Escaping when you had the chance, because if I don't know you, you must have left this godforsaken land years ago. Hell, you could'a ended up like me, or worse..." Motioning to the casket.

"He was in an asylum?" Randy asked.

"Yup. Loony tunes." The old-timer gestured with circles around his ear using a crooked finger, the universal sign for crazy. "But like I said, kid, doesn't really matter. Dear ol' granddad was a leopard!"

More laughter from the man, the stupor of booze had now taken hold. The relative next to him, thinning blond hair yet just as ancient, nodded toward another group. They carried the cackling

13

man away from Randy and the raised coffin. His dead grandfather within those walls forever.

The old booze hound still calling out to Randy, who could only turn back in shock and confusion. The rain beating harder still.

"A leopard never changes his spots, kid! The son of a bitch just got really good at hiding them!"

CHAPTER FOUR

D'elaqua Funeral Home, Mound, Minnesota.

As was common practice in his family, everyone returned to the funeral home for a small token of remembrance. Mound was a small town, but many residents opted to have their relatives buried in the next county. Because most of the elderly people were moved to nursing homes, the younger siblings and their spouses did not want, or need, the bother.

Randy found himself in a room full of strangers. Yes, they may be blood, but they weren't even acquaintances. He had left this dying town for Hamline University in St. Paul a little over a decade ago and never looked back.

A recommendation from his Journalism teacher, who had once worked for United Press International, got Randy an internship with the fledgling paper in Milwaukee. He kept moving upward and eastward, Columbus, Pittsburgh, and finally New York City. Freelancing, because his words flowed, his stories mesmerized.

Journalism was a profession, yes, but his dream, his *great* dream was to become a novelist. To weave stories and tales told, grand adventures into mystery, into awe and wonder. To have his *own* adventures upon the page...but he wasn't there yet. No confidence in himself. Now, confidence in the ring? Bring it! Confidence with women? Hell yes! But not

15

when it came to the words that he loved so much. Not when it came to his greatest happiness. Writing.

And so he took up boxing. Being in the ring with those juiced up behemoths the size of freight trains could maybe, just maybe, grant him confidence within *himself*. Confidence where it mattered most. At least, that was the hope. Hell, he had likely known Jimmy Grillo longer than some of the people here, both young and old.

And he certainly was closer to the gym owner than he was the high and mighty John and Karen Conroy.

His own parents.

And speaking of...

"It's always a shame when a mother has to call her son's employer, just to find out where he is." A dry voice from behind him.

"Hello, Mother," Randy turned, not caring to correct her about his main source of income. One of the few times he had called home--he had needed some old paperwork forwarded to him--this must have been almost nine years back, he had given her Grillo's number as a point of contact.

Assuming she would toss the message in the trash, if she had even written it down at all.

"Oh, good. You remember." Spiteful, but smiling.

Randy gave his mother a kiss on the cheek.

"How could I ever forget this angelic face?" Smiling down at her, his mother was a few inches shorter than he was.

"How indeed," she said, her head tilted up. "But apparently a son will always find a way."

Randy then turned slightly toward his father.

16

"Father," he said, extending his hand. Perhaps a little less kindness.

His father, with a face that was a craggy version of Randy's own, simply turned and walked away toward a group of other men. Like his son, he never looked back.

"We haven't seen you in so long, I can't recall if it has been fifteen or twenty years," his mother said sternly.

You either don't care to remember or want to avoid the realization of how old and bitter you've become, Randy thought.

"So don't you dare make that face!" The way Randy looked at his father. "Since after college, how else do you expect us to react?"

"I've sent you and Dad plane tickets I don't know how many times. Your birthday, Mother's Day, *Father's* Day...." clicking them off on his fingers. "Thanksgiving and Christmas, all first class. You make the choice not to come."

His mother folded her arms and tilted her chin higher.

"Yes, well, you make the choice not to call or write, it seems as if you were the one who made the choice not to care. We weren't even aware that you had moved. At least twice."

Not even acknowledging the fact that she would have gotten the return addresses from the plane tickets sent via FedEx.

"Must be nice living in Manhattan."

"You could always come and tell me, maybe use one of those *tickets*, but then again, with you in New York City, who would be running Hell?" Keeping it quiet enough so none of the other visitors' heads turned.

"You made yourself a stranger to everyone in this room, why should I be any different?" She let her hands drop to her hips. "*Hell*, indeed."

And now a few heads turned in their direction. Conversations had stopped.

"Look, I'm not going to fight with you. You told me to come. And I came." That phone call back "home" that he had eventually made at Grillo's seemed to have gone on forever.

"He was your grandfather, Randy."

"And why do I get the feeling that around here," he motioned to the people now staring, then at his father, "that *that* is less of a statement and more of an accusation?"

"Not sure what that's supposed to mean," once she was mad, his mother drifted away from her fake "polite" grammar. "I'm simply saying that the door swings both ways, is all. You could learn to be a better son."

The deepest cuts always found a way to hurt the most when the truth was spoken.

"Boy, I do hope you come home for Christmas, Ma," Randy stared at his mother. "I do so enjoy these chats."

Silence. The background conversations slowly started up again.

"I saw you talking to Uncle Ken at the funeral."

"Oh, is that who it was?" Remembering him always making scenes during holiday dinners when Randy was a teenager. "Wow, he's gotten--"

"Drunker." A simple shrug from his mother.

18

They both looked over toward where Uncle Ken was propped up in the corner, snoring away. That damn silver flask still angled in his hand, contents staining the beige carpet the color of blood.

"One in every family," his mother said.

"I had an interesting conversation with him," Randy said, disdain in his voice.

"Really now? Well, that's nice, dear." Her inflection had changed again. "I'm happy to see that you're connecting with the other black sheeps in the family."

Randy ignored the barb, the way he might a weak tap to his chest by a tired opponent back in the ring.

"So, Grandpa was committed?" He asked nonchalantly, almost more of a statement than that of a question. Trying to pry open the steel doors that held his "estranged" family's secrets.

Randy's words were like a slap across his mother's face. She put her hands back on her hips, her head cocked back in annoyance. Frustration seeped from her every *Leave It to Beaver* styled, make-up covered pore on her flustered face. Or any of a number of other 1960s sitcoms.

She quickly shook it all away.

"Is that what your uncle told you?"

"Yes, Mother," Randy kept at it, another jab. "That's what my *uncle* said."

"Well, we don't pay attention to him, dear." She stared at Uncle Ken, then at the stain on the floor. "He is a drunk, after all."

"What aren't you telling me?" Randy questioned, words probing, eyes searching his mother's own.

19

She tried so very hard to deflect the talk about Randy's grandfather with the son she hadn't seen in so long, but it was no use.

"Oh, look, it's the Johnson's." She told Randy, gesturing at no one in particular. "Excuse me but I must thank them for coming out in this weather." She kissed him and reminded him to pay his respects--*unfelt*--respects to his grandmother.

Back toward the brown metal chairs in rows along the aisle, two old women in garish outfits were talking about "that handsome young man."

"Oh, that's Karen's son, Randy," the smaller one said.

"That's little Randy?"

"Yes, and I do believe that he's a reporter for one of those big-time newspapers in New York City." And then they set in on how he looked like he came from back East. Or maybe Hollywood. No, the East coast, definitely. Yes, he had certainly shed his good 'ol boy skin for tailored suits that meant big money. And leaving the harsh prairie seasons had only made him look even better.

Both women thought the same thing. He certainly didn't fit in here.

A priest walked around the older biddies, noticing Randy waiting in a short line to pay his respects to his grandmother. Truth be told, Randy was thinking on how it was going to do him a lot of good, seeing as how she was half-dead already.

The priest mistook Randy's impatience with that of grief.

"Hello. I'm Father Malcolm," the bony man said with an easily-rehearsed sigh.

Randy turned at the sound, it was more like an overweight person after climbing a flight of stairs.

"You know, my boy..." he nodded sideways toward where the casket had been earlier that day. "Doctors try to understand this; us, life, all in medical terms. Priests like myself, the church and the Higher Power we represent, all of our denominations try to understand it; Spiritually. But God..."

He laughed quietly. The line toward Randy's grandmother had hardly moved.

"God doesn't try. *God knows.* God knows so we do not have to." He took a step closer. "Sometimes, young man, well, sometimes you just have to stop asking why, and *trust* in him."

Well-rehearsed, the way Randy saw his opponents in the ring, the way he saw older reporters literally "phone in" their stories. The priest laid a hand on Randy's shoulder, believing he was in need of guidance or hope.

"Sometimes we just have to have a little faith." He nodded as his mini-sermon ended.

"Faith?" Randy backed up so that the priest took his hand away.

"Even if only a little," Father Malcolm said, smiling.

"Yeah, well. My grandpa had faith and apparently he was bug-shit insane, a lot of good it did him." Randy didn't care that the priest flinched when he swore. "So next time you see God, you go ahead and tell him to keep his nose out of my business, okay?"

He headed around the line toward his grandmother.

"Matter of fact," he looked back at the tiny man, "why don't you do the same?"

God how he hated this place.

He approached his grandmother, who was in good health but just then was looking about as frail as the priest. He paid his so-called respects the way a stranger might, no love behind the words, and she immediately recognized him.

Randy was hugged, his grandmother's arms not able to reach around his mighty chest. And he listened to her tell of how proud his "Papa" had been that Randy had gotten out--her mannerisms and wordings were pretty much the same as her late husband's had been--and explored the big 'ol world. Had adventures and made something of himself.

How he and his grandfather were so close those many, many years ago.

"It's a shame how time changes things," she said. Telling Randy how, as close as the two had been, the one thing that didn't change for his grandfather was how much he loved Randy, how proud he was of the man that he had become.

"He said that, did he?" Positioning himself away from the rectangular area that had held the casket.

"Oh, yes," his grandmother said. "Very proud."

"Was that before or after he was committed?" He said it quite casually.

His grandmother tried to change the subject, asking him if he had tried any of Aunt Ruth's cobbler. Randy couldn't believe this; *no one* wanted to discuss the final days of this great, this *grand* man's life.

Talk about the past, the war, the family he helped give life to, but nothing after. Not a whisper about asylums, about the madness. Randy mumbled something to his grandmother about the food and walked away.

It was as if his grandfather had become a ghost long before he had passed away.

CHAPTER FIVE

Elder Conroy Residence, Mound, Minnesota.

After leaving his sole remaining grandparent, and a brief stare down with his father nursing a Bourbon 7 across the room, Randy stole away from the rest of his family of strangers. He may have been born here, may have attended grade school and high school here, and he knew that he was not truly a native New Yorker. But being here was like being with a brood of hill people.

He left the room, not once looking back at the relatives whose lives were like the butt of every redneck joke in the book. And then he was gone, just like that.

His rental car couldn't have peeled out of there fast enough. Something just didn't sit right with him. In his mind, he should have been heading back to the Minneapolis-St. Paul International Airport, *back* to civilization. The kind that didn't eat or sacrifice their young while playing banjo tunes... but he just couldn't let it go.

The "why?"

He felt drawn toward something. No...no, he felt drawn toward his grandfather's den. The man was a veteran of the Second World War, a man who had seen firsthand the horrors of life and man. From the beaches of Normandy to the bitter cold of Bastogne, he was a respected hero and man of great strength both physically and mentally. Randy could not believe that his "Papa"--who was so far above everyone else in this godforsaken family--would have descended into madness. No. Not *him*...not him.

Randy would find the answers. And he would begin at his grandparents house.

Randy closed the door ever so slightly and started looking around the room at his grandfather's belongings. Going toward the massive oak desk first, he went through the drawers and then flipped through the dusty books on the back shelf. Knowing his grandpa, clues toward his last days before his death--and commitment, if he still believed that-- were meant to be hidden.

Mysteries meant to be unlocked.

He studied a family photograph, which was a big joke; they all were. The frame was cheap, unlike the easel in the main room of the D'elaqua Funeral Home holding his grandfather's name, his epitaph in a classic calligraphy scrawl. His grandfather was not smiling, and he looked gaunt and pale. Overall sickly. He was seated beside his wife, with Randy's parents on one side and a few of the grieving souls he had noticed at the funeral on the other. The aunt who made the cobbler pie was there, as well.

But what caught his eye was the fact that his grandfather's shirt, light blue with white buttons, was hanging loose off of his left collarbone. The top button had been lost.

And it...

Randy drew the image closer to his face, to the point that his nose was almost touching the glass. From what he could see, it appeared as if his grandfather's flesh was scarred. A marred and pocked canvass depicting layers of--

His ankle bent at a painful angle, Randy realized he had been inching back and to the left as he had examined the photo. He compensated by stepping back and, just like that, he found himself on the floor.

A warped floorboard. No, not broken...it was loose.

A hidden compartment, Randy realized.

A crypt of secrets.

He slowly reached into the crevice, layered over with cobwebs. Reaching down, fingers moving left and right, his grip settled on a ball of clay. He lifted it out and looked at it. Carved into the hard oval was a line-drawing of an old ship. A vessel on turbulent, yet poorly rendered, dark waters.

Randy studied the ball of carved clay, batting away a lone buzzing fly that appeared as if out of nowhere. The object seemed light, hollow. He squeezed it as tightly in his hand as muscle and sinew would allow. First it cracked, and then crumbled into dust and fragments in his palm.

Within the remains of the clay, a safety deposit key glinted dully from the gray that spackled Randy's fingers. The number 15 was etched into the round face. He held the key up to the light from the desk lamp, and suddenly the door to his grandfather's den slammed shut with violent force.

And he could have sworn, for however briefly, as the sound in the door frame reverberated, that he had heard someone whisper the words:

"Get out."

CHAPTER SIX

Sunshine Motel
October 25th, Bright Spell, Minnesota.

Randy sat impatiently and frustrated. He was on a bed in a motel that was better suited for Norman Bates and the corpse of his loving mother. It certainly wasn't a place for a very important, award-winning journalist.

The motel itself was vintage, in that it truly was retro and not a conscious design motif. A hideous shade of vomit green--much like Elvis's Jungle Room at Graceland--greeted whomever the "lucky" soul was who entered this particular room.

The motel was just as repulsive on the outside, as well. Color aside, everything was bolted down. The television was understandable. *Maybe*. Same with some of the "retro" furniture, there was money on eBay for lamps and such, but even the throw rugs were locked tight to the floors, as well as the shower curtain to it's rod in the bathroom.

This shithole sure wasn't the Hyatt, but according to the web search Randy had performed--trying to find a place as far away from his mother and so-called *family* as possible--*nothing* was the Hyatt around these parts. It was just a little too upscale, a little too classy for these good ol' country folk.

It was during that web search that he had spotted this little gem, rated three stars. Funny thing was it

27

was the *only* gem, stars or no stars, in the entire county. The web page had boasted: "From our family to yours, let us welcome you into our home with sunshine."

Hence the ridiculous name.

All it needed was a deformed, banjo-picking mutant, throw in some "squeal like a piggy" locals to more accurately paint the portrait of the motel owner's "sunshine family."

Place should be re-named Motel Deliverance. *Fuck*, Randy thought. *Why am I even here?*

No, the only customers this place received were hookers and couples having affairs. Hooking up whenever they could, *however* they could.

Yeah, give us room 113 please, that's where my best friend's wife and I like to discuss our respective taxes. Squeak-squeak goes the bedsprings, fake "Oh God"s from the prostitutes.

God, he hated this state. And every single person in it.

Animals, he thought, *all of them*. At least in Manhattan, your infidelities seemed classier. Or maybe the fancy hotels made it seem that way. Back home, his *real* home, once you were done screwing your best pal's fiancé, you could then have a nice dinner at a five star restaurant. And let's face it, it *always* came down to the stars. A hundred dollars a plate, double that for their best wine. Ooh-la-la. Enchanté.

Here, again, in this shithole motel 42 miles north of Mound, stars aside, once you were done screwing your best friend's fiancé, you could always go get a Slushy and some beef jerky down the street at the Piggly Wiggly. He had seen one driving up, maybe six blocks back, stuck between a shoe repair hut and a shop that sold Bibles. And, hey, if your car wasn't safely out of the impound yet, that old nasty DUI transgression notwithstanding, you could always walk. Sweaty hand in dainty hand. A nice stroll under a starlit night, might even be romantic.

Animals. ALL of them...Uncle fat ass was right. He did make it out. Just in time.

The safety deposit key was still in his hand, as he sat cross-legged on the bed, which was embroidered with a nautical motif, which went great with the deer head above the telephone and lamp. Never mind the shitty wall color.

Nothing like Bambi to remind you of dear old Mother.

His laptop was open, balanced on a shitty desk that at one time might have been a card table in a homeless shelter. *One* of the main reasons he was so frustrated, family aside, there was no signal. Which meant, of course, that he wasn't able to access the Internet to search for the key's origin. Or, for that matter, the image of the ship that he had, haphazardly, tried to scribble onto a piece of typing paper from memory.

A good journalist never rests when there's a mystery to solve.

Randy found himself making great strides across the room, fed up and frustrated, he slammed the monitor screen down. He turned and grabbed his Blackberry Storm off the mismatched nightstand, a square lamp shade on top of a base that was made out of an old fishing boat's wooden wheel.

Slamming the motel room door shut, he stomped outside, cursing everything under his breath. He must have looked crazy to the locals, which made Randy think, however briefly, that anyone watching could clearly have seen how lunacy must have run in the family. Especially with the show that Randy was putting on.

Come one! Come all! See the big city hotshot meltdown!

He held his Blackberry high to the sky, moving left, then right. Higher, then lower. Tracing invisible squares. Back and forth, this way and that. It was no use, he was in a dead zone. This *entire* county was a dead zone.

No one here even had cell phones, so who were they to judge? Maybe they sold the throwaway ones at the Piggly Wiggly for the truckers passing through. Maybe the truckers would have better luck and get a signal once they fled this godforsaken county.

God how he hated this place!

Randy went to the front desk and a tiny old man greeted him. Pipe in hand, the aroma was actually more pleasing than how Randy had found his bathroom after he had checked in.

"Why can't I get a wireless--I'm trying to get my phone to work…." Randy did his best to keep his voice even. He needed to work on the mystery of the ship and the key fast.

"We don't have any of those fancy computers here," the elderly man said, his thumbs hooked under his armpits. "Which means no cell phone reception, not even that fancy thing you're holding in your hand there. Nope. Not even that."

Randy just stood there, glaring, thinking *where were all the young people?*

"Technology keeps people from living," the old fellow tried to look sage. Talking on how he preferred to experience life and the people within it. That was why the motel was in the middle of nowhere. There wouldn't even be a Walmart here any time in the next decade. His idea of technology was a new adding machine, his receipts were still all handwritten.

Put simply, he didn't want to lose the personal connection people made by interacting with one another.

Yeah, Randy thought. *Wouldn't want that now, would we? God forbid.*

"To hell with technology!" the old man said in agitation.

Randy tried a different tact.

"How many banks are in this town?" he asked.

The only thing Randy *was* able to discern about the safety deposit key was that it wasn't local. Not to the Mound banks, at least. He had questioned, interrogated was more like it, the managers of the two banks before his tire-squealing escape out of town. From *Mother*.

The first bank manager was useless, the second recognized the key instantly, more appropriately the make and model. His bank, he explained, used to have the same kind of safety deposit boxes exclusive to the key's manufacturer before they modernized. There was only one other bank that the manager knew of that still used that kind of safety deposit box that the key had belonged to...and that was 42 miles outside of Mound, Minnesota.

The manager smiled, said that the only reason he had known about the key was not only because he

31

was born and raised in that quiet little hamlet known as Bright Spell, but because he worked eight of his 56 years there before moving to Mound. All Randy heard after that was *blah-blah-blah, yaddah-yaddah-yaddah, bullshit-bullshit-bullshit.*

"Just one," the motel owner smiled, shaking Randy from his thoughts. "It's always been just one."

Well, that narrows the 'origin' down a little now doesn't it. "Well, do you know what time the bank closes?"

"Look, kid." The old man pointed a wrinkled finger at Randy. "Just because I'm the oldest guy around these parts doesn't mean I have all the answers. I just run this here motel, I'm too busy to know what hours those bankers keep. I ain't a banker. Now is there anything else I can do ya for, or can I go about my day in peace?"

Randy walked straight to his car, wishing a heart attack would befall a certain someone, and hoping to get to the bank before it closed. He clicked the door opener, and heard the familiar chirp. And that was when he saw it. Saw...*him*. A disturbing, and flat out frightening old man. Yet he held an air of distinction, and wore an immaculate, crisp black suit and a top hat, straight out of the 1920s, right there in the reflection of the driver's side window.

Hands clasped firmly behind his back, as he moved forward toward--

Randy spun around and saw *nothing*, nothing at all, not man or animal, not even a passing car. He kept his gaze full circle, and saw the motel owner's better half, older than dirt, her bones cracking away in her rocking chair. A mangy old mutt slept beside her, and looked as if he was two seconds closer to death than she was.

Other than the woman and the dog, there was nothing. Just Randy's thoughts on the past that he wished would have stayed buried.

Buried and gone. Where they belonged.

CHAPTER SEVEN

October 25th, Bright Spell, Minnesota.

After a little runaround from the bank manager and some clever thinking on Randy's part, which amounted to a little flirting with whom he had hoped wasn't an underage bank teller, things worked out. That kind of thing never hurt anyone, right? You couldn't get ten to 15 in the state prison just for "talking." *Could you*?

Regardless, charms and looks worked. Randy grinned, said the right words, and made sure the light hit his piercing blue eyes just the right way. Learning from the women of the big bad city certainly had its *benefits*.

Five minutes later he was in the bank vault, closer to the safety deposit box and the secrets it held in its steel trap. *This* was the origin of the key. The box, which once belonged to that grand old man whose name he couldn't remember other than as "Papa," was filled with old photographs, relics from World War II, yellowed newspaper clippings, and a single unmarked hotel card key. No name, no address. Flipping it over, he saw A137 scrawled in crusty red, like dried blood.

One of the smaller items was a business card, dog-eared, for a therapist in West Bright Spell, ten miles down Route 15, by the name of Dr. Douglas Thorne.

34

And among the belongings better fit for a museum than a barred house of cash and heirlooms, was a single image that was sketched, rather poorly as with the other one Randy had seen, of a vessel. A ship steaming forward over dark, turbulent waters. That *same* ship.

But what caught Randy's attention was the fact that, in those dark waters, reaching upward from the depths with clawed, inhuman hands, were shadowed forms. Like ancient man, struggling, fighting, and crawling from out of the primordial ooze. Tearing away fin and claw to become something more. Something *better*.

And upon the bow of that old ship was an old man, the #2 pencil used on the drawing created wrinkles across the face, what might have been a dark suit and what most *certainly* was a top hat, welcoming the shadowed forms below the bow.

An old man that looked very much like the reflection Randy had seen in his car window.

As Sherlock Holmes would say: The plot thickens.

And the game's afoot.

CHAPTER EIGHT

Dr. Douglas Thorne's Office
October 25th, Bright Spell, Minnesota.

Randy was able to catch up with his grandfather's therapist--the first lead he had chosen to follow from the contents of the safety deposit box--as he was leaving his office. Actually, his luck had been pretty good; if he had walked down the hall and to the right, the doctor would have walked from the left and into the vacated elevator.

It would have been a bitch if Randy had missed him, he had driven to the private practice, twelve miles east from the bank on Route 15, bordering the outskirts of the next county. The city of Bright Spell itself was decent, small but with a downtown that didn't consist of just a Main Street. It reminded him of a port town, without the port. Randy would bet that it was relatively crime free here, and amongst the office buildings, a handful stood above five stories.

Such as the one he had entered.

The man Randy had come to see was much older than he was, maybe early 50s, dark hair greying at the sideburns. His hair in general was longer than expected of a man his age. Maybe it was the town's "look".

Randy had asked the man if he could tell him where Dr. Douglas Thorne's office was.

"Well, you found him," he said, not yet holding out his hand. "And you are...?"

Randy told the doctor his name, studying his eyes for any recognition of the name Conroy, and then he followed Thorne back to his office.

"Please, have a seat, young squire," Thorne said in a comforting tone. "And tell me, what affliction has brought you to my humble practice?"

Their discussion was friendly, no assumptions at first, nothing but a journalist implying that he was on a case and a friendly therapist who stuck to the rules of his practice.

Randy was chuckling inside. *Young squire. Affliction.* He'd roll his eyes to the back of his skull if he could. This guy was a real piece of work. He'd never make it in a real city, being eccentric was one thing, but there was something *off* about this man. A little too...peppy. Yeah, that was it. Robin Williams might portray him if the good doctor could ever muster the will to matter to anybody in the real world. Hollywood could care less about 2-D characters.

"Forgive me," was how the conversation had started. "But you are mistaken, doctor. I'm not afflicted, I'm simply looking for information."

"Knowledge?"

"Yes, sir." Randy nodded his head.

"Well then, Mr. Conroy," Thorne touched some papers on his desk. "I am afraid that I am going to be the bearer of bad news."

"How's that?" Randy's smile disappeared.

"The quest for knowledge has been man's greatest pursuit since the dawn of time," still rustling the pages. "When one question is answered, another is asked. Our minds are wheels, Mr. Conroy, around and around they go. See? You *are* afflicted. Lucky for you my rates are competitive."

Randy shook his head in silent laughter. The doctor saw something *familiar* in the young man's eyes. He saw the kid's grandfather.

Their conversation was a pleasant one. He asked about the practice, how long Thorne had been a PhD, things of that nature. Typical interview questions, Randy playing the game. Saying the right things, asking the right questions and breaking down defenses.

It was only as the conversation wore on that he realized that the therapist knew this game all too well. He wasn't just a pro. He was a master.

"Be careful Mr. Conroy. When you fly too close to the sun, the Gods burn your wings."

But Randy kept pushing; a little here, a little there. Impatience creeping into his voice, the way a subtle question became less from the mouth of a caring grandson and more from the lips of a talented journalist digging for clues. Thorne realized this, but said nothing of Randy's charade. He did not suspect that Randy was digging into the life of a man that, as a grandson, he never really knew.

Well, no more games.

"Have you ever thought about therapy, Mr. Conroy?"

"Wow," Randy met his gaze. "What a question. If I didn't know better, I'd say you were trying to up your recruiting quota."

"It's an...*honest* question. No offense meant. Remember, around and around we go. I learned that phrase from an old colleague of mine, Richard King.

He's in Los Angeles now, but he certainly had his pet phrases. Always talking about human nature."

"Uh-huh." Randy forced a smile, that trademark smirk. *Richard King? Human nature? Who gives a shit.*

Thorne went back to a sort of mini-kitchen strategically placed in the corner's nook closest the window. "Offer you a cup?"

"No thank you," Randy said, thinking briefly on the expensive coffee pot. He hadn't even heard it brewing. Certainly it was on a timer. "So about my…"

"I shouldn't even be drinking this," Thorne held the cup high. "I'll be honest, if my wife should see, she'd have a conniption. This will be my, what? Third pot of the day." He inhaled deeply of the brew's wafting scent, and in the faint light of the cozy office Randy could see the tendrils of steam coil out of the cup.

Like something out of a Lovecraftian nightmare. The great Old Ones emerging from the depths. Books he had read as a young teen. And then Randy thought on his grandfather's sketches, drawings of something *else* in that dark abyss.

"Oh, well." Thorne's voice pulled Randy back into reality. "Homestyle Blend has always been my vice. I suppose…well, I know that there are worse conditions."

"I wouldn't know," Randy was showing his impatience. "Now, please. If you could just te--"

"You're probably too young to remember," Thorne said, pantomiming a motion of weighing their respective age differences within his palms. "But there was a commercial where a college

39

student shows up early in the morning at Christmas time. He secretly starts up a pot of coffee. You could tell that the aroma was creeping around the house, waking his parents, surprising them all with gifts and clothing."

He laughed.

"The best part of waking up is Folgers in your cup," he said in a sing-song fashion. "You...familiar with it?"

"No, I'm not," Randy said.

"Ah, well. Great commercial, and I love my coffee." He laughed a private laugh. There was something hidden in the sound. "Although...coffee always keeps me up at night. Now. How have *you* been sleeping since your grandfather's passing?"

And it was then that Randy *finally* understood, he finally got it. He'd give the good doctor this, the guy sure knew how to work a patient. One long tale of Christmas past and right into the question that would set it all up.

"Look at you, Doc," Randy said. "Like a dog with a bone. I don't need this runaround and I certainly don't have time for it. I'm *not* looking to become a patient, so stop trying to get me on your couch."

The distinguished man shrugged.

"Then what *are* you looking for?"

"Answers."

"There's a fine line between madness and insanity," Thorne started up again. "Between *looking* for the answers and searching for the same. And there's a point where a patient must ask him or herself why it is important that they chose one over the other."

There was the break in his defenses, Randy thought, and in that split second moment he believed that he had the upper hand in this verbal game of war. *Fire at will.*

"Yeah, but like I said, I'm not your patient, and we're not talking about me."

"That's interesting that you should say that."

Randy was wrong.

"And why's that?"

"Because I wasn't referring to you, Mr. Conroy, and yet you assumed I was."

He was *very* wrong.

"Then who were you referring to?

"Your grandfather, of course," Thorne said. "I assumed that was why you were here. Or maybe you *would* like to take a seat on my couch."

The man smiled like the devil, Randy thought. *Who knows... maybe he was.*

It went on from there, the two talked, knowing they were in a verbal stalemate. Randy tried to get as much information as possible as the sun slowly set through the large panoramic window behind Thorne. The doctor said that he was not at liberty to disclose his patients, past or present, it did not matter if it was a family member making the inquiries or not.

But he did say that there was a lot of history between his grandfather and him. Randy's grandfather had been seeking Thorne's trust, not only as his therapist, but as his confidant, as well.

Randy pressed him for more answers. He showed Thorne the artwork his grandfather quite possibly had drawn of a ship with no name and no markings, but for the shadowed top hat man and those reaching for the vessel from the dark depths.

Thorne listened, and Randy knew that even though the doctor's reply was vague, he obviously knew something about the image, and certainly knew more than he was telling. *Patient confidentiality*. Ha.

"Your grandfather had a great many demons he wished to exorcise from his past, Mr. Conroy," Thorne said. "You don't see the kind of things that man had witnessed during the war and not come back a little...haunted. But that doesn't make him any less of a great man. He was a hero in my book, and it is a tragedy how his life ended."

"He died in an asylum," Randy said. "There's nothing great or heroic about that."

"Like I said, it *was* a tragedy. And we, young man, are not who we were in the final moments of our lives, but how we are remembered by those we leave behind. Your grandfather was a great man, but just because *his* final moments of life were not, doesn't change that fact."

After their conversation had ended, which left Randy with more questions than answers, he walked toward the door. But before he could leave, the good doctor had a question of his own.

"You know, Mr. Conroy, your grandfather spoke very highly of you."

"So I've been told."

"But he also told me about you and your family's past. You haven't been back to Mound in close to fifteen years now, is that right?"

"And?" Randy had anger building within him.

"I'm just curious as to why a man like yourself, who has no ties to his family whatsoever, no love lost, would even care about his grandfather's past." Thorne took a step toward Randy, eyes narrowing, filled with a sense of awe and wonder, like the curiosity of a scientist dissecting a new life form.

"What are you searching for," he asked.

"What can I say," Randy said after a long pause "I love a good mystery."

CHAPTER NINE

October 25th, Bright Spell, Minnesota.

Why?
Your grandfather spoke very highly of you.
Why?
You're the only one, boy!
WHY ARE YOU HERE!

On his drive back to the motel, twilight setting in, Randy remembered the reasons he left home. Thorne's words stirred up a hornet's nest of memories. Colliding, chaotic.

Randy remembered the reasons he never looked back.

He was close to his grandfather, as a child, as a high school student. He recalled the final moments without goodbyes, thanks to the last argument with his father, how he was slapped across the face so hard that the hand print stayed fresh on Randy's young cheek.

Belongings packed into two bags, harsh words lashing like a whip across his back.

Grandpa suddenly there, eyes red and swollen from lack of sleep. Also from tears, as he saw his own son slap his grandson. Randy had been defensive, thinking *why is this man here?* He thought it was to break down his defenses. Make him change his mind.

No, his grandfather, this grand man, had no idea of the argument ripping through the family. Tearing it apart beyond repair...Grandpa had a different mission. One only Randy could save him from...

Randy thought of another letter received by Jimmy Grillo, words about a ship, a letter from his grandfather asking his grandson to save him before the darkness came back. "Papa" likely holding that letter before placing it into an envelope, like it was not only important to his life, but to all the stars and all the worlds from this one to the next.

Randy could hear his grandfather's hysterical voice, as if it were still screaming. Thorne was right, surely he had been haunted by something. "You're the only one who will believe me, boy! You're the only one who'll believe! I know I'm going mad, but I know I'm not. I'm not. I swear I'm not...please God I swear."

The letter had been destroyed by Randy when he was younger, more bitter, in a fit of anger and what he thought to be betrayal. With rage, he had shoved the letter in his pocket and, on the way home from the gym, he had come across several homeless men, keeping warm near a garbage drum fire. Randy threw the letter into the fire without acknowledging the men.

Fragments. His name on the envelope, the drawing of a little ship on the back. Him storming out of the house, never looking back at those left behind, his cheek still red from his father's slap.

He NEVER looked back.

Not even at his grandfather.

Randy had last seen him kneeling before the fireplace as if he could foretell the future, eyes wild and wide, as fresh tears fell and all his hope...lost.

CHAPTER TEN

Black River Mental Health Facility
October 26th, Black River, Minnesota.

Randy had seemingly come to a dead end in his search for the truth he so desperately sought. There were now more questions; the truth, the *answers* that much more elusive. The images of the ship, the way the door to his grandfather's den had slammed shut, that strange whisper...A warning. A *threat*. The shadowed figures both upon page and then seen out of the corner of his eye.

Foggy memories, *an overactive imagination* he had told himself, but add to that a therapist that certainly had knowledge of *some* sort but was unwilling to share. There were just too many questions with no answers in sight. There was nothing that led to the asylum his grandfather had been committed to just weeks before he had died, in what Randy's imagination and fear had told him was a violent and bloody end.

But him being here in Black River, this where the trail led...and he hoped to God this wasn't where it ended.

There was a part of him, deep down, that felt responsible for his grandfather's death. If only he had listened to the man. The way he had pushed him aside, discarded that letter with such disrespect. If only he could have "saved him."

Maybe things would be different.

Maybe *he* would have been different.

Once he arrived at the mental health facility--it was still an asylum to Randy, no matter what you glossed the truth over with--it was only a few moments before he met Dr. Anthony Midwell, the head of the ward. The man in charge, the overseer of all those sad bastards screaming and clawing and defecating their way to madness.

Midwell explained, once they were in his office, about the strange markings, the artwork and words scrawled across the padded walls and on the floor. Images of ships, of shadowed forms and of a man in a top hat and grin.

Randy showed him the artwork he had found in his grandfather's safety deposit box, asking if it might mean anything. Anything at all.

It was the doctor's hesitation which forced Randy's hand. "What aren't you telling me?"

The doctor gave him the same look that Randy had given Jimmy back at the gym when he had heard the news. It was indifference. It was as if his grandpa was better where he was, buried in the cold, dark earth than out in the open, still alive for all to see. To judge. To *mock*.

"There's all these hushed whispers, these...awkward glances. Everyone at the funeral knew something they weren't saying, and now you," Randy said, with mounting desperation. *"Please* just tell me what everyone else won't."

Dr. Midwell sighed, he knew heavy burdens all to well. Maybe he could spare the young soul his own. "Your grandfather was a sick man, disturbed...He *killed* himself Mr. Conroy, he took his *own* life."

47

"What?" The doctor's words had sunk in instantly, but Randy's shock couldn't be hidden. He *did* care. He cared enough not to believe such a thing.

Midwell said he thought Randy should see something.

His grandfather's room.

CHAPTER ELEVEN

Black River. 2:13 PM.

They walked down a small hallway and took a right turn into a larger one. Once there, Midwell stood back and let Randy dig deeper, studying each image in the room once occupied by his grandfather, as if his *own* life had depended on it.

He took photographs with his Kodak C743, and made spoken notes into a cassette recorder small enough to fit into his back pants pocket. Both sight *and* voice mattered when unlocking the dark secrets of the past. Notes were scribbled and the truth was sought.

It was the journalist in him.

So this is what it felt like to care *again.*

And it was in his unrelenting search for the truth that he found a single image, scrawled with his grandfather's blood. Just as it was after his grandpa had killed himself. This was a crime scene, after all. At one point, to make certain that it was indeed a suicide and not a homicide.

This was where his grandfather had killed himself, and everything was exactly the same.

Midwell told Randy that all of the images, the words and markings were written over the course of one evening. It had been his grandfather's first night in the asylum, and everything had been written or scrawled in blood.

49

They had tried, with no success, to clean the room--*Room, not cell,* Randy thought, *because cell rhymes with Hell*--but the old man had become hostile, saying that everything on the walls was a pattern to the "Other Side," the "Other World."

"Those were his words," Midwell said. "He said the markings needed to be studied and learned from so that others didn't fall into the same nightmare he had."

Randy's grandfather had been sedated and taken away, orderlies scrubbed and sanitized the room. So, there was a shiny, happy cell masquerading as a comforting room for future patients.

And when checked upon the following day, the staff found that Randy's grandfather had turned his new room into the same as the first. The *exact* same images, which told the same horrifically haunting story.

Only one thing was different. The second go-round, the sketch of the ship had the letters Q.M. on it's hull. That was the first clue so desperately sought since the safety deposit box find.

Q.M.

The only thing that mattered.

"Q.M.," Randy repeated, this time not aware he was speaking out loud.

"Yes," Midwell said. "Your grandfather was fixated on it."

"It? You *know* what this means?" Randy pointed at the vessel drawn upon the wall with all that remained of his grandfather's life.

"Yes," Midwell said. "It's the Queen Mary."

"The Queen Mary," Randy repeated.

"Yes. The ghost ship."

CHAPTER TWELVE

Bright Spell Public Library
October 26th, Bright Spell, Minnesota.

Further down the rabbit hole...

Conroy drove over to the town library, in the opposite direction of the motel. He had his cassette recorder and several note pads to help him research the Queen Mary and its dark, haunting and mysterious lore. From its beginnings as a troop transport nicknamed "The Grey Ghost" during wartime, to the decommission in Long Beach, California, decades later.

He learned much about the hauntings that the ship produced during its long history, and each story known had been told countless times over. Hours upon hours of information were searched and recorded on paper and on tape.

Conroy learned of tales such as "Jackie," as well as the fishing vessel that had been cleaved in half during the war, with three hundred souls lost to the seas because the Queen Mary was not allowed to stop for their rescue. Only *two* stories out of hundreds uncovered by his research. From facts to fiction, he wrote it all down.

Endless transcription.

An unending quest.

What *was* he hoping to find?

Certainly not the skeletal old librarian as she walked down the aisle--business hours having long

51

since passed--to send him on his way. But Conroy was persistent in his charm, just as he had been with the young bank teller, he shamelessly flirted with the elderly woman. Tried to worm his way into staying in the library to use its computer for continued research and knowledge.

He would look to the past, before the struggle continued to understand the present.

But it was another nail in the coffin, matching that which was banged into the wood at the motel. The library had no computer.

The librarian was again starting to send him on his way until Conroy told her who he was and why he wanted to stay. Randy was the grandson of a man she had gone to school with back in the day. Her features softened as she continued to listen to his story, his *sorrow and pain*, and after a little more shameless flirting, he was given full access to the library and all of its dusty stacks of books. He simply had to pull the door shut on the way out, it would lock behind him.

"Hope you remember how to use a card catalogue," the older woman smiled over her shoulder as she walked away.

By the time he was ready to lock up, it was the early, early morning. But he had gained reams of knowledge. He had learned so much that even he, a skeptic all the way down to the marrow in his bones, was rattled by the possibility that his grandpa had been onto something.

He was surprised that it wasn't called the Dutchman. Because at this rate, with his luck, his only lead known as the Queen Mary should have disappeared long before he had ever heard the name.

Gotten close.

Unlocked the mystery.

And then it was 3:00 AM. The Devil's Hour.

As he left the table, reaching to click off the old, green banker's lamp at its edge, gathering the last of his research materials, he caught sight of a shadow above him.

Conroy stared at some sort of demonic creature--like some damned hybrid of man and crow, withered and evil--perched upon the piles and stacks of books.

Watching him.

Studying him.

Conroy stood up straight, deja vu all over again, but there was nothing there. He snickered to himself. Seeing shadows within the shadows, his mind playing tricks. An overactive imagination in the day's dawning hours. Nothing more.

Walking back to the research desk, he saw something that shocked him and started his heart racing. *Each* and *every* one of the many books, all of the tomes that he had been researching from, writing down clues all night long, they had all been stacked vertically. Reaching from the table to above his head.

Conroy's immediate thought was that there was someone else in the library. A teenager playing pranks (having seen "Ghostbusters" one too many times no doubt). He turned away from the books and snaked around one aisle and then into another.

"Ha, ha, very funny," Conroy said. "You can come on out now, you dick."

But all he saw was dust and all he heard were echoes.

53

BANG!

The door slammed shut, the prankster gone, having been scared off. Or so he hoped.

He walked back to the desk, now with urgency, and staggered at the sight of the towering stack of books...

They were now piled across the tiled floor, pages torn and spines bent on many, if not all, of them. The chaos of knowledge. Too much destruction for this to have just happened for no reason. Perhaps he had somehow stacked up the books without realizing it, but this? What the hell was going on?

And then he realized that all of the books were shredded, but for one.

A single leather bound book, its pages of aged parchment and dust spread open to one page in particular for him to see.

A lone black and white image to tempt him.

An image of the Queen Mary.

Randy Conroy knew where he had to go.

PART TWO:
EXODUS

"It is a capital mistake to theorize before one has data. Insensibly one begins to twist facts to suit theories, instead of theories to suit facts."

-- Sherlock Holmes,
in Arthur Conan Doyle's *A Scandal in Bohemia*
(1891)

"Fear of things invisible is the natural seed of that which every one in himself calleth religion."

-- Thomas Hobbes,
Leviathan (1651)

CHAPTER THIRTEEN

October 28th, Long Beach, California.

There was a sense of foreboding, an inescapable dread within him. Conroy mused over the chill that ran up his spine and numbed his brain stem the entire flight from Minneapolis to the Los Angeles International Airport. The sense of the inevitable was in him long before he had ever boarded the Queen Mary. Berthed at the Long Beach Terminal since 1967. A towering vessel.

In its shadow lay the mystery of his grandfather's death. Add to that, the strange markings in the cell at the asylum, the box of ragged photographs, the pages of research, the library of parchment and dust, and that single hotel card key. Each clue hidden from the sun, hidden from Conroy, as well. For now.

It was simply the calm before the storm.

He thought of it as a creeping fear wrapped in an enigma upon the still waters of the Pacific. An enigmatic ship, a continent and an ocean away from where it had been built, which, to an overly imaginative mind, seemed to whisper as the waves gently lapped around it. A gentle hush that seemed to beckon you to the dark depths below if you did not respect it.

It.

Ship, vessel.

Steel and construct.

Scientists and medical journals speak of life as being created of cells and DNA, of sinew and blood. A heart pumping, torrents of crimson bringing continued life from one organ to another. Oxygen to feed each of us, flesh to shield us.

All of this. Life is flesh and blood, what the scientists say and what the journals proclaim.

Life is blood and flesh animated by a grey, gelatinous blob of brain matter.

And this ancient--in relation to his years--vessel reaching up before him, the Queen Mary, has supped of the most ancient of blood. Claimed the most ancient of flesh.

Dozens of lives lost since its creation, some during its construction, and many during the pitched battles of World War II when passenger ships and the souls on board were considered collateral damage. There had been rumors of suicides, and of passengers passed off as drunkards falling (or...*pushed*) overboard into cold, waiting waters.

Lives lost to the deep and dark, fathoms leading to the abyssal plain below.

Yes, life is born of flesh and blood. But if that is the case, the Queen Mary has claimed enough lives to be considered...among the living.

Or among the damned. Depending on how you looked at it.

Life has stained its carpets and painted its walls. There is always a dead echo down each corridor.

A *soul*, now. An entirely different tale. A life holds but one, the Queen Mary holds hundreds, if not thousands.

And not all are among the living.

CHAPTER FOURTEEN

The Queen Mary

He could not help but look at the attractive young woman getting out of a Yellow Cab near the main entrance. Her shiny, gold badge read Abigail Marshall. She looked about thirty, if not younger, but looks as they say, could be deceiving. After all, Randy certainly didn't look *his* age. Conroy thought that she had seen more in her lifetime than most others who had spent their days watching CNN or bad reality television.

After all, reality television in its entirety was bad. And only her eyes held the weariness of such sights.

He waded into the Queen Mary, as he passed the young woman. Nodded hello and walked toward the elevator. Just as the doors were closing, Abigail could be seen walking briskly toward them, as well.

"Hold the door!"

They acknowledged each others presence and looked back at the screen of digital numbers. The elevator ascended several stories and then the two went their separate ways. Conroy crossed a small bridge leading him onto the main portion of the ship and he held a smirk the entire way. It was like walking the plank. *Interesting.*

And then the bright California sunlight was gone, no longer warm and comforting on the back of his neck. *He was inside the Queen Mary.* The

59

oppression, he hoped, was just in his mind. Everyone else, those who had been in the other elevators or who had arrived long before he had, walked a lobby fit for kings and were all smiles. He knew that feeling within his gut, the one that slowly churned away, was because of what he was here to do. Because of what he had seen.

He had shaken his head on the cab ride from the Los Angeles International Airport, looking at the sights, *those* nightmarish images of phantom specters, disembodied forms with inhuman voices, and he chuckled out loud. The industrial buildings and the waters beyond held nothing past his overactive imagination. Lack of sleep and nothing more; his mind finding release the only way possible.

His hometown had suffocated him, and he had simply traded one nightmare for another.

"Good morning, sir." Conroy turned at the sound of the woman's familiar voice. She was as breathtaking as the lobby. He again registered the name on her badge. Abigail Marshall.

"Call me Randy," he said. "Randy Conroy, checking in."

She smiled at Conroy. Instant attraction, maybe it was there back in the elevator ride up, but regardless, it would never go past this brief conversation. Chicken-pecking at the keyboard, she watched the screen light up with lists of arrivals and departures.

"Yes, Mr. Conroy," she smiled at him. "We have you down for four days and four nights. Have you stayed with us before?"

He shook his head in the negative, looking both at her as well as the ornate arches behind her lithe form.

"Well," she continued. "We offer plenty of tours onboard, the gift shops and museums are located two floors up, on the Promenade. We also have a number of restaurants, and as you can see across the way, a nice aquarium. In addition--"

"Is there a research area on board," Conroy interrupted. "Books of history, things of that nature. I don't mean from the souvenir shop, more like a library, something like that."

"Besides the tours?"

"Besides the tours," Conroy said sternly. "Yes."

The woman studied him, making it a point to lean as far across the counter as possible to check his clothing.

"You're a reporter?" Eyebrows raised, not so much a question as it was a statement.

This woman could be a handful, Randy thought. And for the first time he looked at her, truly studied her features. He liked what he saw.

"Journalist," he replied.

They shared a smile, as they did in the elevator. Conroy kept his grin a bit longer to offset his rudeness only moments before.

"Ah...New York?" One eye winking.

"That's right," he said. "How'd you--"

"You look like you're from New York," a slight nod of her head.

Conroy thought she seemed unimpressed and asked her if she thought that was a good thing or a bad thing.

61

"Neither," Abigail said. "People come here from all over the world, every day. The only thing that makes it 'good' or 'bad' is how each individual behaves and treats others."

Conroy let that sink in as she continued typing on the keyboard to print out his information.

"So, Mr. Conroy--"

"Please," he said. "Call me Randy."

"Okay," she took in a breath. "So, how is the world these days?"

"Are you serious?" He asked.

"Well, you're the journalist," Abigail replied. "You must see the real side of our news, not just what viewers--myself included--see on the evening news. So I ask again, how is the world these days?"

"Same as it's always been. It's a mess."

"Well, you're the cynic," she said.

"Not a cynic," Conroy laughed. "Just honest."

He extended his hand.

"Randy Conroy. Officially."

She smiled and took his hand. He let the hold linger. Her hands were soft and warm, unlike his own.

"Abigail Marshall," she replied after a beat.

"Beautiful."

"Just the name," she said, self-effacingly.

Wow.

He liked her, he really liked her. She wasn't afraid to call him on his bullshit and certainly didn't seem to put much stock in his name brand clothing or choice of career. Not to mention putting New York and journalist in the same sentence, which would make most women swoon.

Those words together became a desirable balance for hometown hotties and big city cougars, but not for Abigail. Also, she didn't realize how attractive she really was, and that was always a plus. Yeah, he liked her and it showed.

It had been a long time since he had been interested in anyone at all. A long time...

"So you believe the world is a mess, huh?" Abigail asked. Randy couldn't know that she had asked simply to escape his penetrating stare. Because he didn't himself realize how he was looking at her so intently.

God she was beautiful...

Truth was, he was losing himself to her faster than he ever had with anyone else. It must be this place, he rationalized. It had an...*effect* on people. It had to be, he normally was smoother than this. Now he bordered on awkward.

"It always has been," he said. "We just choose to look the other way."

"Wow."

"What?" Randy kept his gaze on her. "It's the truth."

"Depressing much, are you?"

"Says the girl working on a ghost ship."

"The pay is good," she said. "And I love the clam chowder that the Chelsea serves daily."

He leaned in closer, widening his eyes, making them more intense.

"So..."

Abigail followed suit, leaning in slightly, thinking on how this was the most flirtation she'd had received in months. Not by choice, mind you,

Matthew Ewald

she had simply chosen not to participate. Until now. Until *him*.

And she was *enjoying* it immensely.

Conroy's eyes drank in the sight of her. The light sweep of freckles across her tanned face. Pale blue eyes that never wavered from his strong gaze.

"There's something I've wanted to ask you since the first moment I walked on board."

"And what would that be?" Abigail said, still smiling at him.

He smiled right back.

"Seen any ghosts?"

CHAPTER FIFTEEN

5:32 PM, the first night.

Conroy flicked the remote toward the television, hitting a channel at random. He was bored reading the newspapers offered in each cabin room, their pages many and with color photographs accompanying most every article. *The Ocean Times,* as well as another smaller paper, *The Union Jack*, had color photos for the bigger stories.

Flipping the channels from CNN to TCM, USA then Showtime, Sci-Fi or SyFy (whatever they called it these days), Pay-Per-View, then, ahhh, Skinemax and--

The midway point of *The Wizard of Oz* flashed across the screen and he had to click back. It was some local station. A few seconds later, Conroy was staring at the Wicked Witch of the West saying her signature line: *"I'll get you, my pretty, and your little dog, too!"*

Conroy sneered back at the screen. "Why hello there, you green bitch. You what scared grandpa?" then he grinned, swatting at a bothersome fly that was buzzing around the bed.

He then left the room to grab a quick shower before heading out to dinner. He had left a stash of snacks on the chair by the porthole, and he wasn't intending to have his last meal of the night consist of Dorito's and Knott's Berry Farm's Premium Cookies, Raspberry Shortbread. The weight, grams, and calories of the snacks right there front and center to make anyone, not just him, feel bad for indulging.

He barely unpacked; Conroy was used to living out of his suitcase, and after grabbing his bag of toiletries he went into the bathroom and set everything in place around the sink, razor and face wash for the morning, same for the tooth brush and toothpaste. He was impressed by the set-up, the soaps and lotions and the number of towels. The Queen Mary truly *was* fit for a king.

It made him feel even more relaxed, and set in for a good, long and hot shower. He thought about what lay ahead. It was after six by the time he had walked from the steamy room, fresh-faced and hair slicked back, a thick towel wrapped around his waist.

Turning the corner toward his clothes, neat and tidy on the bed, he stopped dead in his tracks.

Looking first at the drawers of the dresser beneath the television, then at the cabinets above them. Swiveling sideways to stare at the closet doors. Every single empty drawer and door was wide open.

Every. Single. One.

And the door was double-locked.

He stood there for a long moment. A very, *very* long moment.

"Well," he finally said. "That's pretty damn disturbing."

CHAPTER SIXTEEN

The Chelsea

Intrigued, but not suspicious of anything staged on his behalf, Conroy took the main stairs two floors up to the Promenade Deck and to the Chelsea, a package at his side. He went over *every* possible scenario in his mind. A reason why *every. Single. Door* and drawer would have come open. He was a journalist, he was *paid* to find answers to questions far more difficult than why simple doors had been wide open.

But ghosts? Come on...that was a little *too* on the nose, now wasn't it?

No...there had to be a more realistic approach, an answer to be found outside of the supernatural.

Randy walked a quarter's length of the ship to reach the restaurant that was sandwiched (no pun intended) between the Queen's Salon and the Royal Salon. All located on the Promenade Deck, Wharf Tower, Elevator Level Four. The sweeping grandeur of the Queen Mary was a sight. Something to *truly* behold. It took his breath away. And then like lightning his thoughts were of Abigail, the lovely girl from the Hotel Registration Lobby.

She had mentioned her love of the clam chowder. Maybe he would, too.

Upon opening the double doors, the first thing Conroy noticed was a huge, framed, maritime map, complete with longitudes and latitudes, and compass

67

headings in a symbol on the lower right hand corner that made him think of a bright star. The map itself was of the Atlantic Ocean.

His heels clicked across the hardwood floor, Conroy noticing glass displays of relics dating as far back as the Queen Mary herself on each side of him. As he waited to be seated, he further surveyed the room. The dining area faced port side, he had read that, just as he had read that on the opposite end of this floating hotel, at the bow, was the Observation Bar. It was a grand lounge, where he was certain that the majority of guests, patrons to be more precise, drank expensive, top shelf whiskey and watched ESPN on a flat screen television that would have run half the length of Conroy's cabin wall.

A hostess soon directed him toward a table for two not far from the door. There were a few other couples and families sitting farther back. The linen at his table was crisp and he could smell the wood around him. The candlelight gave everything a soft glow, a warmth in the darkness. All very relaxing.

"Hello," Conroy turned toward a young man in a black suit, white shirt open at the collar. He looked Filipino. "My name is Dennis and I'll be you waiter for tonight. How has your evening been?"

"Interesting," Conroy said after a few seconds.

"Can I get you something to drink?"

"I'm actually ready to order, thank you." Randy made an effort to scan the menu. "I'll have a cup of the clam chowder, please. And a Diet Pepsi."

"Right away, sir," the waiter moved away to his right and through the crowd.

After briefly glancing at the walls again, Conroy lifted the package; a cream-colored bag from the gift shop, an image of the Queen Mary and the address in Long Beach on one side, blank plastic on the other. He removed a book, the receipt as a marker. $14.95 plus tax.

Flipping through the pages, he shook his head at the photographic proof of ghosts and goblins, thinking to himself, *What the hell am I doing?*

And then, suddenly, he felt it. Eyes. Somebody watching him.

Conroy turned, looking left and then right. And then straight ahead, once another waiter passed, and there she was. Abigail Marshall, sitting at a similar table to his, just a few feet away. A knowing look on her face.

A smile lingering on her lips, then sipping from a bowl of clam chowder.

"Must be fate," Conroy said nonchalantly, not looking directly at her. "Us sitting here."

"Bet that line doesn't always work," Abigail smiled.

"Don't really know, first time I've ever used it. If it *does* work, I guess you'll be the one to tell me."

His waiter returned with a bowl of the steaming soup and a glass of Diet Pepsi. Conroy nodded at him, feeling a bit sheepish that Abigail saw that he had ordered the exact meal she had suggested back at the Registration Lobby.

"I told you, it's the best."

Conroy stood up, carefully holding the bowl in one hand and the bubbling glass of pop in his other, the linen napkin draped over his forearm, as he made his way over to her table.

Abigail made a face, not quite sure what she thought of him yet, other than the fact that she liked his boyish charm. But liking someone and *knowing* someone were two very different things.

"Maybe I could spend a little time with you," Conroy smiled. "For just a little while."

As she watched him set his glass and bowl down, Abigail felt, for the first time in her life, the butterflies that her grandmother had told her about. The ones that floated in your stomach, letting you know that something special was happening.

She shared his smile, and gently offered the chair across from her to him.

"For just a little while," she echoed.

The conversation they had was as filling as the meal, Conroy thinking how there were no more games, just two people attracted to one another. But keeping it honest.

Real.

And from there, it started off with a question of dreams, and like wildfire, like their attraction, it grew into something more.

"So what do you want for your life, your future...dreams?" Abigail leaned in a bit closer, more comfortable being around him now.

The feeling was reciprocated, because, for some reason as he sat with this young woman, he couldn't help but be anything other than completely and utterly honest. Normally he kept this private, something just for himself, but with her...with her it was different. With her it felt...*real*.

So he told her of his *dream* of owning a boat, maybe not next year, maybe not in the next five--a nice size boat you could live on with a bedroom, a full galley and seating area, bathroom and "rooms meant for comfort and solitude," the whole shebang-

-in the Bahamas or down in Florida. A dream of being able to write, he explained, focusing not on journalism, but fiction.

The aspiration of being a real, professional novelist. Writing his words with the endless night of stars above and the equally endless darkness of the waters below.

And he told her of how he would write at night and during the day he would...well, *treasure hunt*. On whichever beach his boat might be docked, at any given time.

Abigail laughed, covering her smile, it was an embarrassment trait carried over from when she had crooked teeth as a teenager.

"Really?" she said, still laughing, which momentarily hit Conroy the wrong way. Though he couldn't know why she had covered her mouth, that her smile was genuine.

"Yeah," he said, and there was a pang of hurt, of embarrassment in his voice. "Don't laugh, I'm serious."

And he was most certainly serious. Abigail saw a dreamer unafraid to dream. Unafraid to chase those stars, as it were. Like a little boy holding onto a dream of going to the moon in a crudely made cardboard space suit, taped and glued and born of his father's empty beer boxes, or a washer and dryer box from the corner lot, if he was lucky.

The capsule. Like the boat he would one day own.

"One day I'll be up there, Daddy! I'll bring you home a moon-rock, Momma!" She could actually hear a young boy's voice air of certainty. But for

71

most everyone--children and adults alike--that "one day" never comes.

But in the case of this man before her, Randy Conroy, she didn't see "one day," she saw certainty. She saw true rarity.

"Nothing fancy with fans or anything like that," Randy continued. "I'm not going to tear up the reef, just...grid and dig, you know. Just enjoy the adventure. Get a dog, a husky, name her Athena. Live on the boat...find a little peace."

"While searching for treasure?" She looked aptly into his eyes.

"While searching for treasure."

There was an awkward silence after that until she noticed the book and gift shop bag. She would let him have his dream of treasures and adventure, but she wanted something in return. She wanted a simple answer as to what was on the table.

So Abigail asked him about the book he had purchased, and about ghosts and specters. Telling him that she didn't really believe in that sort of thing. She had heard of other passengers and crew members talking about hearing strange noises and of, hard as it seemed to believe, seeing things out of the corner of their eyes. The smell of cigar smoke in the old stateroom that Prime Minister Winston Churchill had occupied. The sounds of splashes and of ghostly women in old fashioned bathing suits or dresses. Wet footprints appearing from an empty pool.

Yet she had never seen such things. Never believed.

But for some reason, she mused, with this young man, the wheel always came back around. The topic always found its way home.

Ghosts.

Why ghosts? That was the simple answer she was after. She gazed into those piercing blue eyes, listening intently to his stories and tales, but drifting to a questioning wonder. He was a journalist on a quest to, clearly, unlock some kind of mystery...there was no doubt about that, but to what end? And why here, why the Queen Mary? Why would a man from the opposite end of the country suddenly find *her*?

This wasn't a fluff piece about hauntings--he wasn't even taking notes--it seemed almost...*personal* to him. And she had a feeling, like with most men who came into her life, that he was hiding something.

She knew that Randy Conroy was keeping secrets. She just hoped those secrets weren't as thin as a bed of spider webs.

Well, if he wanted to be a little boy chasing the moon--or in this case specters or wraiths, words she had heard used on television shows that proved that things like ghosts and UFOs and ESP did not exist--she would help him on his little adventure.

Abigail told him that he should take the Paranormal Ship Walk Tour that starts at 8:00 PM on the dot. It wasn't cheap, but maybe with a knowledgeable guide at his aid, he could find whatever answers he was searching for.

"And what makes you think I'm searching for anything?" He asked.

Abigail only smiled, and gently nudged the book on ghosts closer to Randy.

"And what makes you think I'm stupid?"

All he could do was grin and ask if she would like to join him.

"Need someone to hold your hand?" She said, teasingly.

"I'm serious when I say this," Conroy said direct and to the point. "Abigail, come with me tonight."

But she declined his offer, although she did feel attraction. She'd been there before, good-looking guests thinking about quick lays. A piece of "layover ass" as she once heard a guy refer to it.

Although...she had to admit to herself that this "guest" seemed different. Somehow. Regardless, her defenses were not about to be lowered.

"Unless," Conroy said, his tone playful, his eyes seductive. "You're not...*scared*, are you?"

But she declined once more, this time with a little hesitation, telling him that, for her, the stories and tales of the Queen Mary, the legends and lore, were all part of the ship's attraction. She wouldn't deny the ship's history, but that didn't mean that there were lost souls, *ghosts*, still roaming the decks.

"No," Conroy grinned at her. "Just the gullible fools hoping to see one."

And he smiled at her, until she smiled back.

CHAPTER SEVENTEEN

Paranormal Ship Walk Tour
8:04 PM

It was just after 8 PM and Conroy's wallet was fifty dollars lighter.

The Queen Mary's "Attractions @ Night" brochure asked it's owner *what happens when the sun goes down*...and offered four unique and altogether frightening experiences in the form of tours. "The Paranormal Ship Walk Tour" told Randy he was about to *experience the darker side of the Queen Mary* on this guided adventure, while the "Dining with the Spirits," "Paranormal Investigation" and "Twilight Historical Tour" all offered different variations of the spooky.

Not only did they rob you blind with these outrageous prices, but apparently they were going to scare you senseless, as well.

Dun-dun-duuunnn! Randy thought humorously, wondering what the signpost up ahead would foretell, as he folded the brochure four times and slid it into his back pocket against his wallet.

There were about 15 people in his group, it seemed larger because of the close confines of the walkways. Most of the group were wearing shorts and loose tops, a large man in front of him had a loose blue tank top and he was still sweating. It was hot where they were, hot and clammy.

Conroy was in the bowels of the ship.

He had learned more about that little girl named Jackie and another ghost--*spirit* to be politically correct--who haunted one of the stairwells between decks, and how the hottest place--hot as in Ground Zero hot--as far as the ghostly activity was concerned was the First Class Swimming Pool. Several guests on the tour held flashlights and one had a compass, and when they went into the locker room past the empty pool, someone said she smelled flowers and then her friend jumped, yelping that she heard a young man moan.

"Can you feel that warm gust of wind, as well?" From the tour guide, a man not much older than Randy himself, speaking in a dramatic whisper. His community theater troupe must have been on hiatus. "Be *aware*. Be *alert*. The past isn't dead...it is simply *waiting* for us."

Conroy couldn't help but chuckle, as soft a sound as it was it rang loud and clear off the metal walls.

"Something you'd like to add, Mr.--?" The guide turned and shined his own flashlight back toward him.

"Oh, ah..." Randy was caught off-guard. "I'm Conroy, and no, I'm good, thanks, Haley Joel." The last two words a bit lower, referring to the boy actor who always claimed to see dead people in a movie from years back.

"Ah, a skeptic!" the guide moved his flashlight, addressing the entire group. "One in every tour."

Everyone was looking at Randy now.

"And this one," the guide finished, "just volunteered."

He walked a half dozen steps back to Conroy, and took two items from his belt loop. They looked like a primitive set of drumsticks.

"Take these divining rods." He told everyone that the person holding them, the skeptic, the cynic, should see that the rods will turn this way and that, many times pointing directly at ghostly orbs of light. "Now this doesn't always work," he added.

Of course not. "Maybe I should say Abracadabra."

Apparently Randy's charming smirk didn't work all that well below sea level.

"Quiet please and focus."

Conroy held onto the rods lightly at the end, as instructed, and stood completely still. His eyes turned lazy with disbelief as the rod in each hand began spinning of their own accord, he could feel friction on his thumbs and forefingers. Suddenly he felt very cold.

The others around him started backing away, out into the open area. Conroy could feel their eyes on him. The guide was the last one there, he came forward to help as the rods spun ever faster against Conroy's now-whitened knuckles. They were spinning too fast...*inhumanly* fast.

Suddenly, the rods flew from his hands, it was as if they were forced from his burning skin. Shooting outward and upward, the rods stabbed into the tour guide's eyes.

If the man's screams weren't so deafening, one could have heard the laughter.

The very inhuman laughter.

77

CHAPTER EIGHTEEN

Randy's Cabin
"A" Deck, Wharf Tower, Elevator Level 3

Conroy was back in his cabin, splashing cold water repeatedly over his face, over and over. Searching his eyes in the mirror. Reliving everything that had just occurred during the tour. He closed his eyes, imagining the hum of a movie projector.

The audience would be seeing lightning fast, strobe-like flashback images of the tour guide's eyes, turned into empty holes, two pale rods sticking out like the antennae of some hellish half-man, half-insect creation.

Cronenberg would direct.

But he couldn't push the images away, all he saw when he squeezed his eyes shut again were images of blood and terror. Images of sorrow and pain. He *didn't* believe in this shit!

He didn't believe!

My God...what the hell was I thinking coming here?, his inner voice echoed.

But he was starting to, God help him...he was starting to believe. Conroy toweled off his face, once again finding his gaze in the mirror's reflection. His eyes held steady with a growing look of determination.

Shirtless, he stalked back into the cabin, the alarm clock read 2:23 AM. A look of determination

78

made his body go rigid. He reached down to his suitcase, moving aside the clothes he had worn in New York, and pulled on a t-shirt and a long-sleeved shirt over that.

Grabbing his camera, he left the room.

There were no such things as ghosts or phantom specters. Those stories belonged on celluloid and in literature alongside vampires, werewolves, and demons. They belonged in the same fiction as Ghostface killers and babysitter stalkers, hockey mask wearing mutants and dream killing burn victims, in "Fright Night's" and "Plan 9's From Outer Space." They belonged with the trash. His grandfather was psychotic, crazy, mad. It was sickness that had plagued his mind with irrational fears of boogeymen in the dark. *Not* reality. It was sickness.

No. There were no such things as ghosts.

And he was going to prove it.

CHAPTER NINETEEN

The Decks

Minutes later, Conroy was walking the decks, eyes flicking left and right. He took long strides, seeing past the empty night to capture the panoramic, poster-sized images of Winston Churchill, along with other men and women from generations past, making their presence known as he moved the length of the ship. Their sepia-colored eyes, faded from the decades, followed him as he made his way to the Promenade Deck into the dim light of dawn.

He was not chasing after things that went bump in the night, he was looking for answers. *A reason for all of this.* Maybe his grandfather's therapist had been right...maybe he *was* afflicted by his need for understanding. Maybe he *was* being driven by this quest to understand his grandfather's death.

And now, being on *this* ship, walking the decks at such an ungodly hour, hell, maybe he *did* need some therapy of his own. Maybe this was the moment when he should have turned around, packed up his things and left, without ever looking back. Maybe this was the moment when he should have stopped caring.

But instead he continued forward, alone and awake, 3:00 AM drawing near, the flicker of that false dawn on the horizon. Like the glint in eyes seen in old photographs, with the faint sound of music from the 1920s playing overhead.

And *footsteps*. He could have sworn that he had heard footsteps coming up behind him. Conroy quickened his pace, looking left and right. He had his camera primed and ready in his hands. He found *something*, more likely something had found him, some entity that made him know, believe, and find *truth* that he wasn't alone.

Corny? Maybe so, but the truth for him was in that moment. Even if he wasn't that guy. He wasn't like that character Fox Mulder on television with that poster above his file cabinet.

He *didn't* believe.

But there he was, walking down the deck with nothing but music from almost a century before whispering from the speakers. He decided on a plan of action; he'd take two photographs of every image captured. One without a flash, the next with. He would expose the "Other Side" and the light sources that helped to give the "Other Side" life. No flash to deepen the shadows, and then a flash to expose the dead as the fraud that they are. After taking a few more steps, he smelled cigar smoke. Meant nothing to him at all, the portholes could have been opened, might be some guy up late counting his poker winnings.

More footsteps. In his own mind, Conroy heard himself thinking, I'd tell this to someone and they'd say *no way*, my only response would be...*I kid you not. I heard the footsteps of a soul who wasn't there.*

These footsteps were coming up faster from behind him now. He spun around wildly, slightly startled because he fully expected someone to be there. Someone grabbing for his wallet, didn't need to be back in the Big Apple for a mugging. The...*presence*, felt that close. And the camera shutter clicked, but there wasn't anybody there. There was no one.

Randy had taken two photos, as he had learned from his library research. (Yeah, that had been the one good thing about having gone back "home.") But there was nothing. So he turned back around and continued forward. And there they were again, the sound of footfalls, this time faster. A quick turn, two more photos. *Still* no one there.

Conroy looked at the last shot taken and he visibly jumped, almost out of his skin. But since no one else was around, he wasn't going to be explaining it off to anybody. What he had caught on film was one of the most exhilarating and incredible things he had ever seen with his own eyes. This wasn't a photo from an old book or an image caught out of the corner of his eye in the moments between night and day. This was something else.

But he didn't believe!

His hair stood on end as he stood there taking a dozen more photographs, never once catching the same image again. But the feeling he had, the overwhelming dread, that was gone. He had calmed himself down quickly. But he knew what he had seen. And there was the problem, (his mantra) *he didn't believe in such things*, and yet he knew someone was there with him.

He knew that *something* was there with him.

In that one, single photo, there was a shadowed form. He decided almost immediately to call him "Old Salt." From the navy blue peacoat to the white beard with the cigar clenched behind hidden teeth. The shadowed forms of legs walking toward him, but those blurs stopped before reaching the deck.

The bearded man had no feet, no lower legs.

And the bearded man looked pissed as all hell.

Conroy was strong and unafraid, he prided himself on those two traits. But no one, not one single person, would fault him for jumping back four feet upon the sight that was behind the viewfinder. Nor would they fault him for his heart almost beating outside of his chest, or for the nerves that shook his body in what he would later tell himself was adrenaline over fear.

And no one, not any living soul who experienced what he had, would ever fault him for how quickly he made it off the Promenade and back down to his cabin.

Just as no one would fault him for dead bolting the lock...for what good it would do him.

Oh yes, it was as clear as day in the photograph. The bearded specter looked pissed as all hell.

Pissed...at Randy Conroy.

CHAPTER TWENTY

October 29th, Much too early.

He never slept at all that night and it showed. His face was unshaven, and his hair no longer carried the suave and slick coif that he held so perfectly, whether he was typing at his desk or fighting in the ring. And his eyes...his eyes were wild.

He had been up since walking the decks, sitting in his room and examining the photograph. Trying to disprove what it had shown. Trying to understand *reason* behind it. A trick of the lighting, maybe a simple thing like the flash catching the shadow of someone outside, walking the catwalk. But no, no, that wasn't it. The catwalk was further down. Nowhere near where the photo was taken

A potted plant's leaf for the mouth, a steel rivet as an eye...it *wasn't* what he saw. It wasn't...

He left his room for the lobby, and swiftly confronted a clerk.

"What the hell is this?" he said.

"Hello, sir, enjoying your stay?" Trying to be polite, his paycheck depended on it.

"Yeah, this ship is quaint," Conroy had low menace to his voice, "but *what the hell is this*?"

"It appears to be a camera, sir."

"Ha, ha. No shit, Sherlock." Conroy paused. "This! What the hell is this?" Pointing at the image, zoomed in and unmistakable.

"It looks like a photo of the Prom--" The clerk's eyes widened as they focused on the image. "*Oh my God.*"

"You see it too, right?" Conroy's voice carried relief. "Exactly what I thought. So...am I going crazy?"

The clerk finally took his eyes from what the camera depicted.

"Sir?"

"Crazy," Conroy continued. "You know, to actually admit that this ship is fucking haunted. That's what this photo shows, it is *exactly* what this photo shows! Only a bug-shit insane *crazy person* would admit that he saw a ghost last night!"

At this, a few guests turned at his outburst. But Conroy wasn't finished yet.

"And for good measure, a crazy person who caught photographic proof. I mean, that's fucking crazy. I mean, if it worked for my grandfather, why not work for me, right?"

The clerk had no idea how to reply, he was on autopilot. "The Queen Mary has a wide variety of attractions..."

"Dead people are attractions?"

Randy was losing his calm and composure, but it couldn't be helped. His life had taken a sharp turn toward a destination in which he could never have imagined.

...there (WAS) a signpost up ahead...

The clerk stared at the photograph again until Conroy snatched the camera back.

"Look, just tell me where I can find Cabin A137?"

85

After a long moment--the clerk still trying to process what his eyes had seen and his imagination was now giving life to--slid a folded map of the Queen Mary off a pile of brochures toward Conroy. He popped the cap off of his red pen with his teeth, made a cross, and told him that "X" marked the spot.

And when he said that, his voice was a little too cheery, his smile forced. A harsh contrast to the bewilderment and awe that seemed to linger in his eyes. That image had an effect. And Conroy decided then and there that he didn't like the guy. *Add him to the list.*

Just as he also decided that, from that moment on, it was no longer a search for the answers to his grandfather's death, rather it was a hunt for them. He decided in that one moment to start taking this ship more seriously.

Conroy thanked the clerk, in as dry a voice as possible.

"Do you have friends staying in that room, sir?" The clerk remained courteous.

Conroy had already turned to walk away, then his eyes narrowed. His grandfather's card key burned a hole in his pocket.

"No. I have history in that room."

CHAPTER TWENTY-ONE

Cabin A137

Randy checked the plaque on the wall to see which direction he needed to go to get to the room his grandfather had occupied, using the guide map the clerk had given him as reference. The key card from the safety deposit box no longer worked, which was to be expected, but his words and charm still did. *Thank God.*

There was a maid replacing linen in one of the open rooms down the hall, he approached her with ease, telling her that he had left the room with his card key in his jacket pocket. Or... so he thought. He tried to look mildly embarrassed as he patted himself down, still searching for the elusive key.

"I was meeting a friend in the lobby," he added for good measure, "guess I ahhh...forgot it." He flashed a smile, hoped she understood English and finished with, "what do you say darlin, show a little mercy?"

And it was as easy as that.

Where Conroy thought he would find answers, he was left with puzzling contradictions. The room, like the rest of the ship, was perfect. Nothing odd about it, nothing eerie that might trouble a fragile mind. A room.

That was all it was. A room.

No matter how hard he searched and scrutinized, he couldn't find a single clue. That is, until he searched the closet closest to the door, because he knew from experience that small items were invariably left behind on the upper shelf, often unseen by tiny housekeepers. Like the blushing Spanish maid who had let him in.

Conroy had thought he might find a scrap of paper, something in his grandfather's writing, but instead he found that his fingernails chipped away the same crusted color that had been smeared on the key card.

The same--

It hit him like a punch in the gut, like he was back in the ring at Grillo's. It was *blood*. Just as in the padded room, his grandfather was marking the way with blood.

Conroy couldn't get a clear look at what was written there, but by using his camera, the flash illuminating the darkness like a celestial event, he ended up unlocking more puzzling clues.

Ones that would take him into the restricted bowels of the ship.

His eyes studied the image captured by the digital camera, drawn of his grandfather's hand and once crimson life. It was a poorly reconstructed section of the guide map that the clerk had thrust at him earlier. The small plastic rectangular stand that was propped in front of the pamphlets had referred to the sheet as a Self-Guided & Audio Tour Guide Map.

Conroy's grandfather was guiding him from beyond the grave.

He stared again at the image, perhaps a bit too bright from the flash, but easily understood. His grandfather's unwavering finger had recreated the

Immortal Chaplains Sanctuary, a section of the ship on A deck, close to the bow. And there was a determined, bold-stroked X that matched the upside down red triangle on the map tucked away in Conroy's pocket.

An upside down triangle with the number 11 written inside, again in those same bold strokes.

If his face wasn't contorted in determination, and more than a little apprehension, he would have smirked.

But this wasn't an adventure, the clues weren't going to lead him to forgotten relics of old or treasures with an ancient truth which amazed historians and the world alike. Conroy believed that his grandfather believed that he was being stalked while he was here on the Queen Mary. Tormented by an evil poltergeist, some dark entity, take your pick. And, truth was, up until a few hours ago, Conroy would have called the old man, his grandfather (since before the funeral), a crackpot. A nutjob. Crazy...

He couldn't do that anymore, not now. Not after what he'd heard. What he had felt.

What he had *seen*.

His grandpa had stood right where Conroy was now, splitting his flesh and staining a--for the most part--hidden wall, believing the day would come when someone could follow the path laid out. The truth of his grandfather's madness.

And although he wasn't fully convinced that the Queen Mary was truly haunted by spirits and ghosts, being the good little skeptic that he was, he had a feeling that he would find the truth out soon enough.

Because the clerk was right.

X *did* mark the spot.

CHAPTER TWENTY-TWO

"A" Deck

Conroy found his way along the starboard side of the ship--"A" deck wasn't all that crowded at that time of day, evidently--and after a few dozen strides there were hardly any tourists there at all. Matter-of-fact, when he glanced down the long corridor--from bow to stern--there was *no one*. He was alone.

Or so he thought.

He kept up a steady stride, suddenly hearing a familiar voice.

"I heard you have quite the photograph."

Conroy almost skidded to a stop, turning and looking over his shoulder. Abigail was still moving forward; he must have passed by her amidst the throngs and she had finally caught up to him.

For the briefest of moments he was lost to her beauty again, that smile and those weary-yet-loving eyes. The over all calming sense her presence brought. And it was this sedating tone that allowed Conroy to realize that he could tell this woman anything. And everything.

But most of all, and for whatever reason, Randy felt that she *needed* to know. That she needed to know *him*.

And so he started slow, not intentionally trying to build suspense, but slow enough to guarantee that Abigail wouldn't run in the opposite direction--the girl who cried lunatic--when she heard what he was about to say. Hoping that she didn't give him a dose of pepper spray before doing so. He just wanted to spare her any of the grotesqueries, the...*crazy*. And he certainly couldn't lie to himself, it did, it all sounded crazy. But he continued, putting his faith in Abigail where others, if not all, didn't in his grandfather. Including himself.

Abigail listened without interruption as Conroy told her just about everything, not counting the phone call to Grillo's. He told her about the eerie photograph, his learning about his grandfather being committed before his sudden suicide, the funeral and the contents of the safety deposit box. He told her just about as much as a sane person could. Abigail's eyes widened as he described what had happened to the tour guide, and stayed that way even as he backtracked to phantom specters in the Minnesota library and nightmarish reflections in car windows.

By this time, they were in the hotel lobby, and as Abigail finally spoke, things took a darker turn.

"They made this ship an historic landmark," she said. "Bring your family, bring your friends. Take a ghost tour. A lot of people have walked down these halls, but no one really knows their secrets. Their *true* secrets...because no one will ask the questions. No one will dig for the answers. It's like..."

"Like what?" Conroy prodded, looking her square in the eye.

"Randy, it's like they're terrified of what they would find." She laughed then, one that was sad, hopeless and lost all at the same time. He couldn't know of her thoughts just then, but Abigail kept thinking about how much she truly cared for this man she had just met. *Crazy or not.*

Ghosts didn't frighten her. The thing that did scare her? Her attraction for Randy Conroy.

"So why aren't you frightened? Why are you in such a hurry to rush off and follow these clues?" She laughed at the absurdity of it all. "After everything you've seen, everything that's happened, everything that *you've* experienced, why can't you just walk away?"

"What aren't you telling me?"

She leaned inward and took his hand, the touch was electric.

"They're just stories," she said. "You work here long enough and you hear things, people making stories out of sounds, although I don't put much stock in it, either. Sometimes you can't deny what you feel in your gut. Sometimes you can only lie to yourself so much."

She looked back up into his eyes, a different emotion now swimming in their beauty.

"I'm not saying the ship is haunted...but there is something here. So I'm asking you. Let it go. This is a truly beautiful ship, but there are miles of dark and nothing else far below us. Don't lose yourself in it."

Although her attempts to warn Conroy of the dangers that lay ahead might have failed, she wasn't about to give up on him. She understood that he was unfaltering when it came to this quest to unlock the mysteries surrounding his grandfather's death. The mystery of that dark character in the top hat who had driven the old man to madness.

He would not fail his grandfather again, she knew that.

And, in turn, she would not fail him.

And so it was that they both continued to a sanctuary whose name held several meanings.

Together, they would brave the dark.

Together, with caution in each step, they continued forward into the limbo of this phantasmagorical world.

CHAPTER TWENTY-THREE

Immortal Chaplains Sanctuary

Stories and tales told. One clue leading to another. One clue leading to a sanctum that Randy and Abigail now found themselves within.

The Immortal Chaplains Sanctuary was dedicated to the memory of four chaplains, each of different faiths--Jewish, Catholic, Methodist and Protestant--four men who had given up their own life jackets, their very survival, so that other soldiers may live. These chaplains remained with the 672 men who perished. They remained together through fire and cold, through bloodshed and screams. They were Four Immortal Chaplains last seen arm-in-arm in prayer as the U.S.A.T. Dorchester, a troopship, was torpedoed and sank into the cold, merciless waters of the North Atlantic on February 3, 1943.

The Queen Mary was also a troopship during World War II. History would say that she was the most successful of the war, having carried close to one million soldiers into combat.

But that was not all she carried. The Queen Mary carried U.S. soldiers, as well as the crew of the German U-Boat 223 which was responsible for the sinking and destruction of the U.S.A.T. Dorchester the very year before. She carried the souls and memory of the dead.

And as Randy and Abigail searched the sanctuary for the clues his grandfather had left

95

behind--sanctuary or not, they were searching for the dead--Randy wondered which lost souls of the past were awaiting him in the darkness, this madness he found himself within. He wondered why his grandfather would desecrate a sanctuary meant to honor and protect.

As he stared at another image, stained by blood and hidden from sight, presumably pointing the way to the answers Conroy so desperately sought, he wondered why those answers were pointing the way *down*.

He wondered why they were pointing to Hell.

Created in two sections, with the first depicting the deepest level of the hull, was another poorly recreated section of the Queen Mary. A location circled, but, as with the notation on the guide map in Conroy's back pocket...a void of nothingness. The outline of the ship and nothing more. A white square on a beige colored map.

The second image was that of the deepest level of the hull, but there was no void, no emptiness there. Instead there were bodies. Hundreds of bodies were crawling upward in the bloody image, smashed together tight. Trampled. Stacked. Sickly.

A Nazi swastika had been carved into each and every forehead, blood in all directions, from unseeing eye sockets to matted hair and contorted mouths. But that was the least of it. There was the specter in the top hat, his grin large, spread out across his haunting, blood-stained face, welcoming them from the bow with open arms.

Etched from a mad memory, broken nails and fingerprints of blood. The vessel, full steam ahead.

Blotches that represented children all made up to pose with rosy cheeks and sad faces.

Like little dolls.

Eerie, persistent...two tiny words to express what the image conveyed, but it did however serve its purpose.

"Oh, my God!" Abigail exclaimed, her eyes widening. "*I know this.*"

"What? *How*?"

She backed up slowly, looking from the ragged red image, then up at Conroy, still unaware of how badly she had fallen for him. Back and forth, back and forth, a metronome of the fear lingering in her eyes. And she suddenly connected another piece of the puzzle with a stark and startling realization.

A separate part of the whole that she had never even realized she held, just under the surface. Like a body in the water.

"Abigail," Conroy said her name as calm as he could. "How...?"

Silence. Sounds around them faded out, as if the two of them had been submerged. Conroy didn't have time to ponder the irony of that, because Abigail spoke just then.

"Your grandfather told me."

CHAPTER TWENTY-FOUR

Immortal Chaplains Sanctuary

And with those four words, Randy Conroy learned the terrifying truth behind his grandfather's past, the verity of someone who had been here, not the snickering statements of relatives two time zones away. He'd learn why the man he'd called grandpa had been haunted by the vessel known as the Queen Mary and of the ancient evil that lurked within its bowels.

He learned with a story told, that the darkness which had plagued his grandfather in his final days, that *same* darkness, had been making itself known to *himself* the entire time.

Abigail had a look of concentration on her flawless face, as if trying to recall every detail before starting the story. No, not a story, she sighed, rather the terrible facts.

Her shift had ended, it had been a long day, added work to the normal routine. As was the norm for that day, she headed to the Chelsea for dinner, for the soothing bowl of clam chowder that would ease her weariness. It was only after she ordered that she took notice of the kind, older man she had helped check in only a few days before. He had been alone, his only luggage a small bag that could easily have doubled as a carry on from whatever flight had brought him to Long Beach.

He didn't have a suntan, and she seemed to recall that he had mentioned Minnesota and its many lakes and cold winters. Laughing at her insistence that he had an accent when, according to him, he most certainly did not.

Ya sure, ya betcha and what're you talkin a'boot?

Abigail remembered that he had praised his grandson up and down, made him walk on water. *He's a talented writer*, he had said, smiling. *Made something of himself.* They had talked until new guests waiting to *journey back into time and enjoy the authentic and unique experiences offered on this majestic ship* made them part ways. But he had been adamant that a woman of her beauty would fall for his grandson.

Imagine my undeniable charm and good looks in a younger body, well, that's my grandson.

He had said it in a joking way, and Abigail had replied with something like, well in that case, how could she resist? And with that, he was gone and she was on her way back to work. She didn't see him again until a few days later.

Only that time, he had been sitting there, crying at his table, clutching a rosary so tight. He was begging the Lord, pleading to St. Jude, worker of miracles, helper of the hopeless to hear his prayer. To *help* him. A lost soul tormented. It was as clear as day.

She had approached him and offered an ear and a beautiful smile, but what he had told her caused her worry. What he had shared with her and her alone caused her next few nights to be restless. Why he shared that story with her, she didn't know, and

99

never would. But it wasn't the story that terrified her, it was the fact that he had believed.

And when the story was told, *she* had believed it, as well.

The Curious Case of the Arrival and Departure of one Mr. Thetepet

Back in the day, once released from her service during WWII, the RMS Queen Mary--known as The Grey Ghost during the war--ferried war brides and children to the United States and Canada before returning to service as a trans-Atlantic cruise ship.

During the War Brides Tour the ship had picked up her passengers in port and steamed forward, all engines ahead. But it wasn't long afterward, while out at sea, that the reports had come in of three children gone missing.

Parents had panicked, and rightfully so, demanding answers. And then the fourth report came in, yet another missing child. A little boy, last seen playing near the First Class Swimming Pool area.

And the search began. Cabin by cabin, deck by deck. As the minutes stretched on, it became terrifying for all those onboard. To the parents of the little ones feared lost, and to those who clenched their own little boys and girls tight, fearing that they might also suffer some unknown fate.

Panic became terror when--finally--they found a man sitting ever so quietly, like a true gentleman, in the tight confines of the engine room. An immaculately dressed man, wearing a top hat, sitting very calmly, a grin from ear to ear with four dead children propped up beside him like dolls. Their faces smiling with rosy cheeks, but eyes contorted in panic-stricken expressions.

And as the crew reeled back in horror, the man in the top hat simply sat there, eerily quiet, even as they pounced on him. Beating him and restraining his bruised and bloodied flesh.

Eerily quiet, until suddenly requesting an audience with the Captain. He asked as casually as one might say good morning. The man in the top hat and the haunted grin told the Captain that he was respectfully requesting another half-dozen *children. No more, no less.*

The Captain was appalled, letting duty dictate action instead of the rage boiling within him.

"Who are you?"

The man replied with only a name, Mr. Thetepet. Not Mister, he made a point of accentuating the fact that there would be no period in his name. And then

Matthew Ewald

he repeated the words that he was but a humble collector and that he had a quota to fill.

The Captain ordered that his crew check the ship's passenger manifest, only to find that there was no one with that name. An unaccounted for. Men were dispatched for a head count.

The man with the top hat sat quietly through it all.

The manifest held hundreds of passengers, names, date of births, and the Captain stared at the one man who should not be on board. A stowaway, perhaps. Or something...else. The Captain did not know, but he certainly would, he'd be damned to find out if it was his last duty as commander of this ship. To make certain that this man received the punishment he deserved.

The man in the top hat went willingly to a cell found at the deepest depths of the Queen Mary, until he could answer for his sins. A deep black pit of steel that had held German POWs during the recent war, the man was now in a prison of darkness.

Word had spread quickly and the parents of the children who were safe breathed a sigh of relief, but the parents of the children who were brutally abducted demanded retribution. They demanded blood.

The parents and those who believed in the justice that should be meted out then and there, stormed the lower decks, roaring into the bowels. Dragging the man in the top hat back into the light. His damnable grin never faded, not even as they beat and tore at him, ripping flesh from bone, and finally castrating him and spilling his blood in a torrent of anger and rage.

And as the parents and their accomplices, for several crew members wanted justice served as well, strung a noose around the man's neck, not yet dead, he smiled and gave a gentle bow and then there was a sharp crack as he was tossed over the Sports Deck balcony. The snap of his neck could be heard over the ocean waves that lapped against the massive ship.

The line was then cut and his corpse continued overboard, falling to the darkened, cold waters below. No one assembled would ever breathe a word of it. Nothing ever happened, children were lost tragically, but justice had been dealt swiftly.

And yet the man in the top hat would become a grinning catalyst. A beacon of despair. No one, not passenger nor crew member, realized that it was only the beginning.

Conroy's grandfather was a young man then, empowered by the loss and rage of the dead children's parents. Their cries for justice heard and acknowledged in the only way he understood. It was he *who had led the charge,* he *had tied the noose, beaten the flesh and kicked at the bone.*

He spat in the face of the darkest evil he had ever witnessed and he had cut the line that delivered that evil back into the black depths from which it came.

And many, many years later, with children of his own and children of their own, he was still haunted by those violent ends, and the fierce end he had dealt in the name of justice.

But there was a price.

There was always a price.

103

Something was happening as he aged, his past so vague and long ago. He was an old man now, nearing the end of his life, but something had come for him. Something he thought forever lost to the past. A man in a top hat and grin. A darkness tormenting him and claiming his sanity little by little, piece by piece.

Conroy's grandfather became obsessed; he came to the Queen Mary for answers, to rid himself of this demonic poltergeist which stalked him to the point of madness, but also to warn those who would follow in his footsteps. But upon doing so, the torment became worse. This was long after he had gone to Randy for help, the only one who would believe, but, as he cruelly discovered, there was nothing left of that family. He was alone, his own wife looked at him as if he were a circus act, a freak in a cage. A shadow.

Until she looked at him with fear at the events that haunted their home. Being dragged from his bed in the middle of the night, scratches and bite marks appearing on flesh. Lamps and furniture inhumanly thrown across the room by an invisible force. This thing of madness had driven them apart. The love of his life now just as afraid of being in the same room with him as she was before crawling into bed at night, as she was of being alone in the darkness.

Waiting and wondering what would happen next.

Praying and pleading that nothing would.

Randy's grandfather was the conduit. He was the link.

And it was only until hearing Abigail retelling the story his grandfather had once told her that he understood how far reaching this nightmare was.

Randy's uncle, Ken, wasn't a drunk out of laziness or escape, he was a drunk to make the nightmare more bearable. When Randy's grandfather had left his home and wife, "to save them from such nightmares" he stayed with Ken, thus unknowingly inviting another victim into the darkness. And oh did this evil have fun with him, oh yes indeed.

In the end, Randy's grandfather battled the darkness the best he could, from mental cleansing to therapy, from a type of exorcism to prayer, but the darkness was patient and it held no bounds. It would drive him to spill his own blood. And it would promise that it would achieve its quota even if it meant taking his children and their children's children.

For they would suffer the same fate.

And, in all honesty, who would say a word about these supernatural events? Who would admit to such things? So the family buried their history, their "experiences" just as they would one day bury that once grand man known as "Papa." And on that day, they would forever forget his nightmarish past. And on that day they would never look back.

And it was in that moment, that he, as a storyteller, would finally understand the given clue that he had been trying to decipher for all those many, many years. Who this Mr. Thetepet truly was.

And little did he know the answers he so desperately sought were right there in front of him the entire time, simply never understood. Never unlocked, never known.

A clue deciphered by the young woman sitting at his table.

Mr. Thetepet.

It was an enigma, she had told him. A riddle within an amalgam.

An anagram.

Mr. Thetepet.

It meant The Tempter.

It was another name for...The Devil.

CHAPTER TWENTY-FIVE

Sun Deck
Starboard Side

"And this ship is still steaming, Randy."

Conroy stared at Abigail without blinking.

"Full speed ahead on oceans of flesh," she finished the tale, but not before adding one final echo of a dead man's words. "He had been adamant, the way he spoke to me. You think its going to stop for you or anyone else, he asked? This ship may be dry docked, but a part of it is still out there on those dark waters of the Atlantic. It's been that way for decades. And it will be that way long after we are dead...That's what your grandfather told me during our last conversation."

Someone nearby was telling a group of people to move in closer for a group photo.

"That's what he told me *here* on this ship..."

The two sat in silence for a long moment after that. They had moved, retreated from the Immortal Chaplains Sanctuary and into the light of day after Randy had documented everything that he could of the bloody image in photographs and notes.

They had retreated from the horrid and haunting images of the death and despair that Randy's grandfather had created, and now found themselves sitting quietly upon a red bench angled next to the Hollywood Deli and Arcade. They were overlooking the calm, blue waters of the Pacific from the Sun Deck, but Randy was anything but calm.

How could his grandfather have known that she would have seen the blood created image? How could he have known, all that time ago, that these two would have ever met? How could he have known Abigail Marshall would have followed his grandson into the darkness, into the black of Hell and shared his story? *How*?

Was it destiny or fate? *Faith* perhaps? Was it a precognitive truth or was it simply coincidence? Happenstance...a stab in the dark? Two young souls who just *happened* upon one another? What was it?

But what Randy also had to ask himself was what if it wasn't his grandfather orchestrating this quest of mysteries...what if it was something else? He had to acknowledge that, just as he had to acknowledge that if he was a puppet in this nightmare, then who or *what* the hell was the puppeteer?

And could it truly be the devil?

Conroy was haunted by the words which had come from her lips and were formed by her tongue. And he knew that Abigail was still terrified by her *own* words, as well. Mortified at the connection that now linked the two of them together.

She admitted to Conroy that she had told herself back then, talking with the seemingly harmless man, that it was just a story, but now she didn't know what to believe. She had followed the clues with the young man at her side. What had began as harmless flirtation and the strongest attraction she had ever felt--though this part she kept to herself, embarrassed to say as much--had become something different. Something frightening.

To believe in Heaven is to acknowledge Hell.

And just as Conroy was beginning to truly understand the scope of the horror that was facing him, the two of them had to part ways. Abigail had to report for work and he himself needed to get a few hours of sleep.

Because tonight he had a demon to catch.

CHAPTER TWENTY-SIX

Promenade Deck
Wharf Tower, Elevator Level 4

It was closing in on three in the morning, and Conroy stood on the Promenade Deck. He was ready this time, prepared, having done his research because, compared to that shithole motel back in Minnesota, the Queen Mary had a decent Internet connection.

To which: *In European folklore, the witching hour is the time when supernatural creatures such as witches, demons and ghosts are thought to be at their most powerful, and black magic at its most effective. This hour is typically midnight, and the term may now be used to refer to this time of night, or any late hour, even without having the associated superstitious beliefs. The term "witching hour" can also refer to the period from midnight on, while the "devils hour" refers to the time around 3am.*

It was a mouthful, but he didn't care. He didn't need words right now, he just needed this nightmare to end. And tonight he was going to do just--

Conroy was startled by the sound of laughter. The playful mirth of children. He spun back and around, using the fighting stance he was long familiar with, and searched the shadows for the first time since stepping on board the vessel. Suddenly, he was again unsure of his own sanity.

He moved deeper into the ship, there was no sound but for the faint music overhead. There was nothing there, nothing but his frosty breath in front of him. A few hours before dawn in late October would make it cold even if the ship was docked in Puerta Vallarta.

But this was different than last night. This was oppressing.

He could feel...he could feel *death*.

The laughter grew fainter, then louder again as Conroy moved faster, running from the thickness in the air for the staircase that would lead him from the Promenade to the Sun Deck.

But just as he reached the top of the stairwell, the wooden railings cold, his feet clanging on the metal steps, something struck him hard from behind. His legs caved in and he tumbled back down.

Hands were now wrapped around his throat, catching the hair at the back of his head in a way that made Conroy's scalp go taut. Laughter drowned out all other sound, and he was being violently drug back the length of the hall. He swung his arms and his fists as if he was *indeed* back in the ring, but all his hands caught was air. There was *nothing there*.

He charged for the main hall, making his way quickly past the WWII display and the small Passenger Information Desk when something again slammed into his legs, spinning him like a top before knocking him to the ground.

Children.

They were children...their faces made up to look like demonic dolls, laughing and giggling, pulling at him. Coming into full focus, spinning around him, holding hands. Circling him like a pack of wolves.

111

Kicking at his body, their inhuman teeth chomping at his flesh. It was all happening too fast, too sudden for him to react properly.

What were they? Demented visions of the dead? Was it a battle for sanity or truth? Visions of the past, ghosts of the present? Dementia dominating a gruesome end he would soon face?

What the fuck were they!

He fought through the wide-eyed fear that had claimed him, his sanity in check simply because if he didn't have any fear, well, then something would be terribly wrong. Conroy pushed at the children, bodies exploding in puffs of vapor, then reforming, tendrils of smoke reaching out like symbiotic organisms. Like a fog off of the Pacific, a disembodied malevolence twisting over the hardwood of the Promenade Deck. A thick curtain alive in the darkness. Solidified bodies, haunting grins. Soulless eyes. They were still slapping and striking at him, kicking and thrashing, laughing the entire time.

They were *enjoying* it.

And then, suddenly, footsteps replaced laughter. Footsteps that made the phantom children stop as if an OFF button had been pressed. Tears and looks of terrible fear on each of their painted faces, blood staining the wooden floorboards, as they all adopted mannequin-like poses. Unmoving and silent all around Randy.

Lifeless.

Yet they all smiled big, cheerful grins, it was only the look in their eyes that told the true tale. These echoes of once-living children, these waif-like specters felt terror, they knew dread and Conroy could hear "its" approach with every step, as it came nearer, step by step, on the wooden floorboards.

He turned just as the phantom passed, the man in the top hat. Mr. Thetepet. Its face was death, more teeth in his frightening grin than humanly possible, the edges of his lips curling upward into a deformed Cheshire Cat-type swirl. His eyes found Conroy's, like embers in the starlight. Like hundreds and millions of pinholes in the curtain of night, but instead of locking on him, he never stopped. He simply continued forward with a nod of his "topper", letting him know that this was only the beginning.

And that there was *no* escape.

And there never would be.

CHAPTER TWENTY-SEVEN

Promenade Deck

A drunk. The man before Conroy, a patch on his sleeve reading Queen Mary Security, was thinking that alcohol had made this man a fool. Some kind of fight over a bar tab, no doubt. Maybe a skirt.

"So, how do the other guys look?" The guard chuckled. "And um...where did they go, exactly?"

"They, ah, he..." This was all Conroy was able to sputter, it was impossible to catch his breath. He was beaten and bloodied, terrified out of his mind. He couldn't stop his eyes from blinking, and his legs wouldn't stand firm.

After a few seconds of staggering, he regained his air of authority. He was roughly the same age as the security guard, a wannabe cop on domestic detail, he sure as hell wasn't going to let the man think him an idiot.

"I need to talk with Abigail Marshall," Conroy said. "Can you please take me to--"

"Hey," the guard said, snapping his fingers. Getting back the attention this glorified ex-mall cop thought he deserved. "Stay with me, okay? Where.,,

Did.

They.

Go?"

"They just, they went..." Conroy's finger was crooked and pointing at the wall that separated the deck he was on from the Queen's Salon. He didn't know that the guard still thought he had been slapped around by other guests. It had happened before in a long history, more than once.

"You saying they walked through the walls?"

Conroy *had* told him that, he had said it as soon as he had seen the guard, when blood was still dripping down his forehead. The guard was taking it all in and kept looking in the direction where Conroy was pointing.

And then he laughed, leaning in close to Randy, his flashlight shining into his own face for dramatic effect. A campfire tale to haunt.

"Come on now, son, nothing just..." he paused dramatically, "*walks* through walls."

CHAPTER TWENTY-EIGHT

Randy's Cabin

Back in his cabin, Conroy couldn't stop his hands from shaking. He was told to *sleep it off*, but he simply sat there, every noise startling him. The television was no longer muted, he could hear a sultry woman's voice, a late night XXX celebrity suggesting that the viewer would get quite a bit of enjoyment by calling an eleven digit number. Letting him know that he was in the real world, no matter if it was made out of plastic or silicone or real flesh and blood.

He hoped that the guard had taken him seriously and that Abigail was on her way.

His damn hands. Why couldn't he stop his hands from shaking?

Conroy felt like a fool, a damned fool, as he slid off of his bed and dropped to his knees. His hands were now held tight, fingers laced together, no longer filled with an uncontrollable tremor.

Yes, he felt like a fool, but he prayed nonetheless. For the first time in over a decade, he was asking for help from all that he had turned his back on after he had left home.

For the first time in his life...*he believed.*

"Our Father," he began, "who art in Heaven,
Hallowed be thy name.
Thy kingdom come,
Thy will be done,

116

On earth as it is in heaven.
Give us this day our daily bread,
And forgive us our trespasses,
As we forgive those who trespass against us.
And lead us not into temptation,
But deliver us from evil."
Amen.

Matthew Ewald

PART THREE:
THE DEPTHS

"We wait for light, but behold darkness."
-- Isaiah, 59:9

"[E]very time a savage tracks his game he employs a minuteness of observation, and an accuracy of inductive and deductive reasoning which, applied to other matters, would assure some reputation as a man of science[...T]he intellectual labour of a 'good hunter or warrior' considerably exceeds that of an ordinary Englishman."

-- THOMAS H. HUXLEY

"Abandon all hope, ye who enter here."
-- Canto III

CHAPTER TWENTY-NINE

October 30th
Closer to the edge of reality.

Abigail was straddling him, gloriously nude and looking at him as if the secrets of the universe were within the radiant blue-grey of his eyes. She would devour him. She would know the universe's secrets.

She believed this, so he believed.

But wait. This...this wasn't right. Abigail wasn't there.

Conroy was praying, *imploring* for salvation, for guidance and deliverance. He remembered, as if in a dazed moment, closing his eyes, and for just a moment he confirmed with himself, telling his every muscle and nerve not to feel helpless in the darkness of his cabin. Not to let his guard down.

He had to stay alert for what he *knew* was coming for him. So he promised himself he would only rest his eyes, and not let the quiet solitude of sleep claim him for even a second.

Reassuring himself, as strongly as he did all those many years ago when he vowed never to return home. And then his grandfather died. And then he had to break that vow...

So here he was in an empty bed, the sheets like satin against his skin. Soft, warm, and oh so inviting. Like her lips. Abigail's lips. The taste of her mouth, her skin...that look she held when she talked with him. Like she expected him to know the secrets of the universe. Secrets in the darkness.

He saw crystals and ancient races, long gone from this Earth. He saw horror and love, wishes and desires; and the hopes, darkness and torments of every man, woman, and child. The way he knew what a star *felt* upon its birth.

No. No, he didn't know any of that. His mind held the mutterings of a madman.

This was wrong. What was happening to him?

And if Abigail was there in front of him, how did she get in? Of course, he didn't care. For all he knew, she palmed a key card from the front desk. She was now his, the deadbolt secured, the gilded chain linked to the frame...

...so how did she get in--but then she was staring down at him, moving above him, the sensation making his eyes roll back into his head. And then they were making love. He was her God. Giving her all of himself; every fiber, every molecule of his being. Conroy loved her. He loved all of her and she loved all of him.

Completely. Entirely.

But why was she looking at him like that?

Why was she suddenly made up like a porcelain doll? Cheeks the color of rose, a smile as fake as the doll that she cradled against her breasts as she rode him unceasingly.

And then maggots and black bile flowed from her mouth in a torrent.

Something clawed at his legs. He heard knocking, something was knock-knock-knocking at his skull, hands were at his feet, then under the covers. Rough and raw like parchment covered in veins, pulling at him now. Abigail was gone *(no, don't go)* he needed her, her kiss, her smile, her love...but she was no longer wrapping her Lilith form around him, staring at him with her lambent eyes.

She was crawling on the walls. Her stomach splayed open like a Venus flytrap, teeth and all.

Knocking.

Invisible hands tore away the sheets, his legs were held and he was being drug off the bed, slamming into the thin carpet with a harsh thud. Carpet stains grinned at him. Mocked.

What the hell? The man he had fought in the ring was standing over him, beating on his skull with his massive fists, a spectral Grillo cheering him on like a champ. His tattoos grinning at him, like the stains. Moving underneath his skin, pulsating and undulating with some semblance of a sickened life. The dragon hissed, its forked tongue like lightning licking at the earth itself.

Knocking...

The fighter was knocking his teeth out with those demonic children snatching them up like they were on an Easter egg hunt, presenting each bloodied piece of enamel and ivory proudly above their heads for the Tooth Fairy and the many prizes they were promised she would bring.

His mother was scolding him from the corner of the hotel suite for spilling so much blood on the carpet, he had always been such a messy...*child*. She cradled a deformed mutant of a baby as she did so.

The walls undulated with thousands of flies. The collective buzzing was that of the bell in the ring, muted from too many direct hits to the head. And then...

The man in the top hat and grin was sitting in one of his cabin's chairs, playing a violin. *Cell rhymed with hell. A fiddle of gold against his soul.* For his mind was becoming a prison in which there was no escape.

...knocking...

He was knocking his head against the floor, hoping to spill out his brains and end this--

KNOCKING.

Randy's eyes shot open, sweat was dripping off of his body as if he had just done three miles on the treadmill at a speed of seven-oh. And he was on the floor. On the floor, hands still locked in prayer. Sunlight was streaming through the lone porthole of his room, igniting his world from the darkness.

The knocking finally stopped, the door swung open and Abigail's face was in view.

"Randy? Are you in there?" She didn't see him in the darkness right away. *"Are you all right?"* Sounding frantic.

From the angle, Randy could see that his cabin's door was slightly ajar, her face racked with worry and pressed between the small crack, peering into the room, searching for any sign that Randy was safe. She must have abused her power as a Queen Mary employee and made herself a key to his room when he did not respond to her calls. *Just like in his dream,* only he didn't think about that now. She was a tribute to worry. And she needed him, as he needed her.

"The deadbolt is chained," she continued, "I can't get in, you need to answer me!"

124

Did her voice just quiver?

A dream. It was all just a dream and Randy was on the floor, praying. People pray in dreams, right? They pray, play ping pong, watch "Battlestar," fly through the night skies and swim through the dark waters. Apparently nightmares were inescapable onboard the Queen Mary. No matter if you were asleep or not.

Once Abigail entered the room, her fears had proven to have not been totally unfounded.

"My God what happened to you?" That same quivering tone.

The previous night's ghostly attack had left his body bloodied and scratched. He hadn't cleaned himself up yet, upon entering the room he just fell to his knees, and he just...prayed. He just prayed.

"We have to go." His voice was strong, even. A mission of intent.

"What?" Abigail had calmed down, and had brought tissues and a cold wash cloth to touch his bruises. Calm the nerves. "Why? Where are we going?"

Randy ignited the beam of his flashlight, before sliding it into his right back pocket.

"Down," he told her. Letting it sink in. "We're going below."

Abigail explained why this just couldn't happen, telling him that the below decks, those *dark depths*, from the locked doors of "A" Deck and all of "B," to those farther down, the sub-levels, the engine room, the rust and darkness of all the places on the Guide Map that were a white void of beige and nothingness, were ALL off limits, locked and secured. There were only two or three keys which opened those doors, and once opened, the tour guides were trained to lock the doors up securely behind themselves. It was routine, but *no one* was allowed access to those areas. No one.

"I *need* to get down there."

"Randy..."

Her hands were on his face and he betrayed himself from the mission, because he lost himself in her touch. Conroy closed his eyes, a comforting warmth and calm enveloped him immediately. Abigail gently smoothed the bruised and soft flesh below his eyes, and combed her fingers through his unkempt hair. She placed her cheek against his.

This must be what love, real *love feels like*, he thought.

And as she pulled away, her hands still on his face, but now searching his eyes, she smiled.

She had calmed the beast inside of him.

She had stopped whatever darkness was dancing on the flaming ashes of his soul.

Or so she thought.

Conroy leaned forward, cupping Abigail's chin in his hand.

"Abigail...I need you to do me a favor."

CHAPTER THIRTY

Sun Deck
Hollywood Deli

Randy and Abigail had something in common long before they had ever met, they *both* knew how to work a room.

And so it was that the woman Conroy loved so much acquired the needed information with a quickness that surprised even him.

She had gone up to see one of the ship's "Ghosts & Legends" guides, who had just finished placing an order for a sandwich at the Hollywood Deli on the Sun Deck, her hands coyly folded behind her back, throwing in a fidgety look for good measure.

Oh yes...she certainly knew how to work a room.

"If they find out that I let you borrow this, especially after what happened to Derek," he shook his head, thinking about the tour guide who was now hospitalized with little hope of ever seeing again, "*I* could *lose* my job."

"It will be Our. Little. Secret." Abigail had kept it playful. Her smile had been radiant, her cleavage adjusted with the proper prominence.

When she had related the story to Conroy, he was thinking *Hey, tour guide! What color are her eyes? You know, up here, big guy.* "Fine, fine," the man had told her, "but if anyone catches you with this--"

127

"I won't *breathe* a word of this to anyone," she said, interrupting him from continuing his admonishment. She took the key from his trembling hand and slid it into her purse, tracing delicate fingers across the guide's lanky chest. "If anything, I'm persistent."

Poor guy...

Yet, regardless of her shameful flirtation to get what she (and Conroy) wanted (and needed), a trick learned when puberty struck and high school rolled around, everything worked out just fine.

She wanted to make Conroy happy, because she saw the look in his eyes, *Randy's eyes.* The wild and almost frightening determination. And with the item stashed away in her purse, she knew he'd be happy, and that made her feel the same.

The two of them with a key between them, something that would deliver him into the heart and darkness of the Queen Mary's dark underbelly. Places no tourist was ever meant to see.

What she hadn't told him, was that as she headed for his cabin, she questioned whether or not that once he had descended, far below the dark waters, if the darkness...once it had him...if there would be anything left of him to return.

Anything at all.

CHAPTER THIRTY-ONE

Randy's Cabin

He had been excited when she had retuned so soon, in fact, Conroy barely had a chance to make mental notes or try to detach himself by watching CNN or something lighter like the newest season of "PSYCH." But he still did not notice the feelings she had concealed so well. Journalist or not, he was blinded by her. She was a mystery all unto herself. The perfect hunter to his damnable prey.

"You got the key that fast?"

"I..." Abigail hesitated. Why was every single fiber, every essence of her being screaming that she not hand over the key? Why did she know that if she went below into those depths with him, true believer or not, that something bad would surely happen?

"Abigail," Conroy looked into her eyes. "Did you get the key?"

She kissed him then, hard. Her eyes might have been closed tightly in passion, but his were wide open, feeling her tongue slowly slip between his lips. It didn't take long for him to surrender to her. To give himself over to her completely. The perfect hunter.

All thoughts of ghosts and entities, the demonic nightmares of what cursed things dwelled below decks were gone. Vanished in the haze of passion.

And so in the minutes before she finally told him the story of her talk with the tour guide, Abigail realized that she loved Randy, and she also knew that he truly loved her. Others might call it too sudden, too soon. A fairy tale love brought on by attraction and nothing more. Yet she knew with her own heart, she knew that it was right, that it was *true*. She knew her heart, so she would do what she must, with body, lies, and/or deceit in order to protect him. In order to keep him safe from whatever it was that was within this ship. Human or not, she would protect him from...from *it*. She would make him forget this business of ghosts. She wanted him regardless, she wanted *this*. And the price of his safety was a price Abigail Marshall was more than willing to pay.

More than willing.

In mind, body...and soul.

CHAPTER THIRTY-TWO

Randy's Cabin
Hours & Ecstasy Later

Conroy had slipped the key from her purse, the key he *knew* she had when Abigail's hesitation spoke.

He had slipped the key from her purse, because there was no way he could let her follow him. Not to where he was going...not into that kind of darkness. Not to those depths.

He realized this as they had made love, more times in those hours than he had with anyone else in his lifetime. They had explored each other as new lovers did; Conroy found her body as smooth as a river stone and she had found his as fulfilling in her every need as humanly possible.

And when she drifted, only after believing he was already fast asleep, exhausted by passion and intensity, he left her there, naked in his bed, covering her long legs and generous breasts out of protectfulness, even though he knew no one else would be entering the room after he had left.

He rummaged through the privacy of her purse, secured the key, and left for a place he did not want her ever knowing about.

That world was now his life, a world of phantom evil and where legends and lore became truth and certainty. This was his world now, and he would protect her from it.

131

Even if it meant protecting her from himself.

That is why he took the key.

He wasn't stealing from Abigail. He was *saving* her.

Stories and tales told were one thing, but truth, and the *sights* behind them were something else entirely.

She was trying to protect him, save him, with her hesitation and passion and, well, he would *protect her* by leaving her behind. For this nightmare was one that he had to brave alone. He loved her. She made up his heart...his *perfect hunter*.

So like Dante, and with no hope or expectation of being guided by Virgil, Randy Conroy strode into nightmare.

And into the inferno of hell.

CHAPTER THIRTY-THREE

The Long Walk

Armed with only his courage and a Mag-Lite he had packed deep within his luggage, its battery power quickly draining--Conroy suspected, and there would be some who would say rightly so, that spirits and paranormal activity drained energy in order to cross over into our realm--he continued out into the black with a light that dimmed ever so slowly.

And like his torch, slightly arcing with each sway of his form he slowly moved down the length of "A" Deck. His eyes adjusting to each new pattern of an era's authentic carpet and classic decorum. His fingertips touching one another, reliving the sensation of Abigail's naked skin. Like a young man going to enlist, apprehension and nerves screamed. Like a last meal and a long shackled walk, fear at the unknown twisted his insides to sickness. Slowly he was passing the Lobby Bar and then the "A" Deck Passageway to the Hotel Registration Lobby.

Slowly, ever so slowly, he was then passing the restrooms and there, up ahead, he could make out the bend in the ship leading to the Immortal Chaplains Sanctuary and it was then that he found himself by two wooden double doors, secured tightly, and motionless now like his own body.

The restricted area was locked, just as Abigail had said, and the darkness welcomed him as if he

133

were coming home. The first ring of Hell opened its jaws and howled.

Easing the doors closed tightly behind him, resecured with a twist and a turn of the "borrowed" key, he moved cautiously into the darkness.

How many steps had he taken?

How many turns?

Through how many hatches and corridors to get here?

Were the bread crumbs in his mind as precise as the Guide Map in his back pocket?

One-hundred and twenty-nine steps forward, duck through the hatchway, veer slightly to the left, go down a flight of rusted metal stairs.

New deck. New depth.

Sixteen steps ahead...keep going...just keep going.

And he never looked back. Not once. Not even as he replayed the tour guide's opening words over and over in his mind as he descended into those black depths.

The past isn't dead...

No, Randy knew that it wasn't...

The past wasn't dead...

It's simply waiting for you.

CHAPTER THIRTY-FOUR

The Lower Decks

What is fantasy?
What is reality?

Flies were buzzing around Conroy, making him into a new life form of sound, the buzzings' cadence lowered as he slowly made his way deeper into the ship's lower decks.

He had remembered this location, where the unplanned safety drill had resulted in a hatch being slammed on a young engineer, crushing him. It must have been, what? Seventy years ago?

There were other stories, *many* other stories that remained clear in his mind, stark realities of this and that, a homicide here, a sad and unexpected accident there. Spread over years. Decades.

Everything that he had etched in his mind from the newspapers he had read just days ago.

And yet, with the exception of the one he had come to call "Old Salt," he hadn't had any encounters with the souls that this vessel had devoured as its own.

Yet, that darkness had now seemed to have set its sights on him, marking him as its own. A plague of blackness that had devoured his grandfather's sanity and now had set its sight on him. Yes, *marked* as its own.

Randy Conroy belonged to *it* now.

135

Maybe that was why he had never seen, never encountered anyone or...*thing*, other than "Old Salt." No orbs, no cold spots or curious odors. Every spectral possibility knew better. Mr. Thetepet did not share. *This ship*...did not share. Randy Conroy was off limits.

Like every single fly, all of them trapped in the depths of the Queen Mary. They all belonged to the steel.

The other things that Conroy needed to address would have to step aside and wait their turn.

The entity that was now using the name Mr. Thetepet had *tempted* Conroy this entire time. First, he had claimed his grandfather, but not before eating away at the man's sanity. All the time steering him with each haunting, each sudden reveal out of the corner of the eye until he was aboard the Queen Mary. It was a slow game. A game of thorns. A carrot and a stick was far too subtle, follow the bread crumbs of souls...

So was Conroy following the clues that his grandfather had left, or did this *devil* make him believe that the dead man's scattered warnings were the clues?

He didn't know. At that moment, it didn't matter, none of it did. He was here now, a traveler in a nightmare funhouse. He would not turn back until he found a way to appease this evil, or until he found a way to kill it.

Harker had his vampire. Holmes his Moriarty. Arthur the very blood and lineage in his veins. Victor Frankenstein his monster...Conroy had the devil.

136

He didn't hold that thought for long. The ghost children were back, and this time they were singing.

"Flies in your eyes!" The children sang, dancing as they ushered him deeper down this damnable path.

Conroy found himself in a maze; he had lost track of direction.

"Flies in your eyes and the dead man's cries!"

And the dead man's cries?

Well, those belonged to his grandfather.

CHAPTER THIRTY-FIVE

Deeper

Alive.

He was alive, but in a terrible way.

Conroy's grandfather was hanging upside down on a cross that was fashioned from the steel and rivets of the Queen Mary, rusted and cracked. The implication being that this makeshift cross had been there for decades. "Papa" bound by the same noose he had securely fastened around the neck of Mr. Thetepet those many, many years ago.

It was madness...it was *all* madness and nightmare. Like the madness and nightmare that Randy felt tearing at his cabin walls. Those same cabin walls that separated his sanity and soul from those that existed *within* the darkness of this ship.

Yes, it was all madness and nightmare...regardless though, the stench was that of death. *His grandfather's death.*

Conroy watched in horror as the children laughed and danced around his grandpa, and then, those little beasts, abruptly stopped.

Motionless forms and mannequin poses. Windup dolls stopped dead. It was as if they were presenting him with the gift of his grandfather's crucifixion. The elder man's mouth was agape, forming a perfect "O", larger and longer than humanly possible, but the screams were silent. Yet Conroy could hear his grandfather's screams clear in his mind. He was sharing the pain of his own personal hell.

This was the price of his suicide at the hands of a devil.

And it was at this very moment that Conroy knew that something was behind him. Someone. No. Some *thing*.

It was Mr. Thetepet, it was *the devil*, and as if in response to the sudden chill in the air, the ship groaned loudly. Groaned, as if in pain.

Groaned out loud, as if it was a warning for Conroy to run. As if the battered hull of the Queen Mary knew that the devil would get his due, as he had done many times before.

CHAPTER THIRTY-SIX

*October 31st*
Sometime after midnight.

Abigail woke up with a smile on her face, and she could tell how radiant that smile truly was by the deep breaths that filled her lungs. The happiness, the warmth of blushing cheeks and upper chest, like a secret meant only for herself, but one she could not keep from the world. And as that radiant smile widened, she delicately covered her mouth. She desperately wanted to suppress the giggles that came with the realization that she was incredibly *loud* during her lovemaking with Randy. Loud enough to wake the neighbors. Loud enough to wake the dead.

But she didn't care. She was happy. For the first time in a *long* while, she felt her eyes no longer weary. Her heart no longer burdened with heaviness. For the first time in a long while, she felt...*free*.

So this *was love. True love*.

Abigail turned, pulling the sheets higher, her barely-covered modesty held in check, as she draped an arm over...

...an empty sheet.

Randy!

He was gone and she had jumped out of bed, not caring for her nakedness as she searched the small cabin. Her left foot was tapping an uncontrollable beat, adrenaline lacing her veins. Abigail's eyes widened in desperation and now her entire nude body shivered.

And then she knew...

Truth was, she knew the moment she draped her arm over the memory of the lover who was no longer there.

And then the fear became very, *very* real.

She looked across the small distance of the space that made up Randy's cabin. She looked past the bed with its covers and pillows sweaty and strewn about--the aftermath of passion--and to the deadbolt undone on the door she herself had locked securely the night before.

But it wasn't the deadbolt she was truly focused on. It was her purse slumped beside that door.

She didn't need to search its contents. She didn't need to feel around for the key...

She knew.

She wasn't mad that he had left her, that he had gone into that hell alone. Oh, no. She was angry at the possibility that she herself wouldn't be able to kill him first for doing so!

Please, God, she found herself praying inwardly, as she threw her clothes on in a rush. *Please, God, bring him back to me safely.*

Please God, just let him be all right.

CHAPTER THIRTY-SEVEN

And Deeper Still

Conroy charged blindly, going deeper--being *driven* deeper--into the ship.

He charged past miles of piping that soon resembled German soldiers. Those Nazis screaming in their native tongue what must have been curse words, opaque tears in their eyes, as Randy passed and fought back their clawing fingers and outstretched arms. Their war wounds gaping and spilling out black life. And it was these echoes of the once-living that were *fused* to the Queen Mary, in the walls, the pipes, the flooring. Part man and flesh, part rivet and steel. A damnable merging in a steampunk hell, one seamlessly becoming the other. Cogs turning, steam expelling upwards into the darkness, screaming Nazis expelling a defecation of bowels, of bile and gore everywhere else.

Whatever it was that was pursuing Randy, the devil or not, that presence was no longer there. Nothing gave chase. Once Conroy had struggled his way through that mechanized purgatory which had produced so many horrors, he didn't have to run anymore.

And the thought made his stomach churn.

Regardless, he *couldn't* run, couldn't even jog another step. The path had been lost and now terrible visions of sorrow had replaced it.

Hundreds of body bags loomed mountainous before him. And all he could do was climb.

He pushed through the piles that were stacked so impossibly high in this endless hell, so deep that to Randy time was un-spooling before his very eyes, like a film projector spewing out tape in a heaping pile at his feet. It was like he could feel himself falling into darkness' cold embrace. Vertigo and black. Everything blurred, the world spun, and he was falling...falling deeper. A never-ending spiral into oblivion, hearing nothing but his own heartbeat and the zipper's teeth pulling apart.

Wait...WHAT?

The zipper on the closest one moved slowly downward. Whatever---*whoever* it was inside--wanted out. In the worst possible way.

"Mom?" Conroy mouthed the word as he saw the bag fall away from his mother's familiar visage. Her cadaver naked with the bluish, pale grey of death. Autopsy incision unstitched and splayed open wide, her insides rotting and wafting a terrible stench.

"You've let us down, Randy," her voice, just as he had heard it during the funeral. "You could learn to be a better son."

Then another zipper, another bag.

Conroy knew who that would be, he envisioned this as easily as he could Abigail's naked body wrapped in cool, comforting sheets back in the hotel room.

"Why did you leave us?" a semblance of his father asked. "Why did you fail me?"

And with that, Conroy knew that he didn't have to run anymore. He didn't have to climb or charge or fight any longer...no, he didn't need to run.

He didn't have to run because he knew that he was heading right to where the darkness wanted him to be.

CHAPTER THIRTY-EIGHT

RUN!

Abigail charged forward, weaving through the long corridors of "A" deck. She dodged several sleep deprived stragglers and one group of college roommates, looking older than Randy did, that had their luggage piled everywhere. One voice trailing as she left them behind, words and excitement of wanting to experience a *real* scare in a haunted spook house. Other voices, so faint now, saying that there was *no* such thing...

She hugged the main lobby's grand staircase of decorative wood carving and beauty and headed down as far as she was legally allowed. Legally, until she violently slammed into one door on "B" deck which reverberated with her forceful impact, but did not budge...not even when she fought against it with all of her might. Which also meant that she didn't give a damn about breaking rules. Not now. Not when it came to her love.

Sprinting across the hallway, she once more climbed that grand staircase back to "A" deck and then fresh air suddenly filled her heaving lungs. She knew that her actions were drawing looks from both guests and crew alike, but she didn't care...she just *didn't care*.

Let them look, let them talk, just please...please let him *be okay.*

145

Moving faster, she charged across the Outside Gangway and then whipped down the stairs toward "D" Deck and the ground level. More looks, more attention as she ran across the parking lot--her feet slapping on the pavement, hair a wild mane, a tangled mess of strands--and then she was taking another staircase toward the "Ghosts & Legends" entrance. If any doors would be unlocked, it would be them...

It *had* to be them.

Her eyes held a pleading look as she ran toward the double doors ahead, charging forward even still. They were the doors that would deliver her, just as they had done for Randy, into the deepest level of the Queen Mary.

Let the doors be open.

She was close now, fingers reaching. Hand splayed forward.

Please, Randy. Tell me you left them open.

Closer still. Fingers tightening.

Please God, just let them be open.

The muscles in her arms tightened as well, and she struggled against those double doors leading into the restricted areas of the ship. She pulled with all of her might.

OPEN!

But those doors...were locked.

No. Please God no.

Please...

Secured tight.

The afterglow of lovemaking no longer radiant upon her face; all that was left for her to know was fear.

Unmoving. Unrelenting.

And the despair of knowing that Randy was alone down there. So *deep* below those dark waters.

She thought of the man she loved being not just physically alone, but also alone with the darkness that she now knew to have truly existed. The devil was real. And it wanted the man that she loved for itself.

She realized that he was alone...

And abandoned.

CHAPTER THIRTY-NINE

The Void of White

Randy Conroy. Writer. Fighter. Chronicler.

He had come face to face with evil and barely escaped with his life. With his sanity. It wasn't the *true* evil he had faced, not yet at least, but it was all close enough. That other evil, well...that was still in pursuit. *He* was still toying with him.

And just when he remembered what it was like to feel safe, be it off the ship and in full daylight or in the shadowed-yet-comforting embrace of the woman he loved, he came to realize that a darker truth awaited him.

A truth which, deep down into the very essence of his soul, proclaimed that he had now become the devil's prey.

It wasn't just toying with him. It was *hunting*.

But even here, deep below, even with all of this darkness surrounding and stalking and demanding his soul, he could still feel the heat of Abigail beside him. God how he longed to hold her, just hold her hand in his...

Just...

Conroy shook the thoughts away. Abigail was safe; he wouldn't think of her here, not...*here*. Regardless, it didn't matter, she might as well be have been half a world away. Just the thought of having her join in this nightmare set his teeth on edge, half a world away or not.

He knew that she would disagree. Of course she would. He knew *that* much, she would say that she should be there with him, protecting him. But, no, he wouldn't risk her in a place like this.

He would *never* risk her...

And then he had lost track of time, again, and suddenly stumbled in what was once a location that seemed to be an area where old parchment had been kept, perhaps logs and employment records, certainly maps and charts. There even appeared to be a small stack of novels and *Time Life* magazines halfway between deepened shadow and forgotten memory. It all smelled like the dust of a retirement home.

Upon closer examination, Conroy saw that it was a storage room, mismatched furniture and books stacked in rising columns, old relics in clumped piles on top of battered cabinets. And there in the midst of the room, the demonic children were sitting, their faces turned down toward pages of yellowed paper, reading quietly to themselves. Apparently play time was over.

Each shushed him as he passed a couch, a chair, a bare cushion...

His grandfather would have called the old parchment in their chubby little hands "research documents." But research on what? Conroy might have thought this, not that long ago, as he trudged down more stairs toward another unknown room, the void of white. The faint flicker of his Mag-Lite in the darkness his only company.

Research on it's history? The ship, it's crew...the dead? he thought with fresh perspective. *No...no, leave the dead where they belong.*

He was getting close, he could feel it. And then when something in the dark struck him in the face it became a certainty that he had arrived at the destination he had been looking for.

His right cheek was split, and he was certain that his flesh could be found under the fingernails of whatever it was that had clawed at him.

"Get out!" a demonic voice screamed from nowhere and from everywhere, but Conroy was still half-dazed and confused by the sudden strike.

Wake up, damn it. Wake up!

But this time it wasn't a dream. No, it wasn't even a *nightmare*.

It was something *far* worse.

A heartbeat later, just time enough for an eye to blink, that *something* grabbed Conroy hard by his shirt and launched him across the room.

He sailed into one of the many book shelves after bouncing off of one of the file cabinets. Once a secure sanctuary of fine literature, tomes and file folders fell unceremoniously to the dusty floor. Conroy's body followed, now lying in a rubble of age-old knowledge. The shelving swayed from the impact, curled press clippings thumb-tacked to frames wavered side to side.

Rows of filing cabinets, untouched and unnoticed for years--as was evident from the three inch thick piles of dust, but for the one Conroy banged across--had their drawer's jarred open from the impact. Contents spilled to the floor, WWII photographs, smiling couples on serene waters, the documented construction of the Queen Mary herself, it was *all* a war zone in a matter of seconds.

He reached for the Mag-Lite, and gripped it tightly, shining it into the darkness. Pointing it toward--

--a shadow moved, dodging the beam, and Conroy realized that the flashlight, the *light itself,* was a weapon. He pressed on, pushing the shadowed thing toward the farthest wall, he was gaining an advantage. That is, until yet another demonic entity roughly grabbed his jaw, studying him with shadowed eyes. It reminded him of the scene in "Predator." Only this time the credits wouldn't be rolling shortly afterward, but he feared his obituary would be...

"It's youuuu," the voice dragged the syllable out, and like an E.V.P. Conroy heard static in his ears. *"Heee liiikes youuuuu. And youuu muuust runnn."*

"Fuck you!" Conroy bit out in defiance, fingers clenched tight around the flashlight, glaring at the shadowed form next to him. "Fuck you, and *him*, *all of you*!"

He spat in the shadow demon's face, but it did not land nor insult, it did not anger or enrage, it just sailed away into more darkness...

So instead, he swung the flashlight in an arc, the beam striking the shadowed thing in what, he assumed, was its face and it exploded into a rupture of crows that cawed and swarmed upward and away from the light.

And with that, the other shadow was gone, leaving a low, primeval call to the Tempter--the one it considered it's *Master*--and it's brethren of lurking darkness within the parallel of this life. The "Other Side."

151

And it was only after the darkness called back, that Randy Conroy heeded the shadow's words.

CHAPTER FORTY

The Nightmare of "G" Deck

"RUN!" The voice in Conroy's head screamed and echoed at the same time.

The hail of primal rage poured out of the darkness like a horde of locusts that followed on his heels as he sprinted across the room in another steel encased hell beyond "D" Deck.

Obscenities came out of his inhuman pursuers in guttural growls, exploding like fire, spraying molten slugs that were once steel and iron at Conroy. If not for his fighting skills, he would surely be dead. A dodge, a leap. *Head body, head body...*

Keep moving!

The creatures, whatever they were, *unclassified* in any book, *ancient* beyond years, or perhaps simply *unknown* but for what they held of the knowledge in the paranormal, were a hair's breadth from dragging their talons across the delicate perfection of the lifeblood that coursed in Randy's throat.

And yet the creatures were just getting started. With a rumble and a roar--

--the *real* nightmare made itself known.

It was the sound of thunder.

It was the sound of an *entire* world dying.

And *that* sound was deafening.

Randy's ears were ringing; a high-pitched tone flat-lining in his head. It was a resounding

153

thunderous splitting of the earth, echoing from the cry of the demonic predators giving chase.

"Oh God Oh God Oh God!" Conroy's cry might have been considered a little *less* threatening.

He charged down new steps, knowing full well that he was descending further into the darkness of "F" Deck. He had no other options. Not even as he tripped over the bottom steps--his flashlight, his only weapon against the darkness, met steel, shattering it's lens--and skidded to a halt just past what he believed was another long corridor that would lead him to "G" Deck. Its length of steel and catwalks bathed in a soft crescent light caused by his weapon's broken lens.

It was the kind of lighting that could make the dead seemingly crawl from out of their graves. As if it commanded the darkness to *open it's jaws...and HOWL.*

"Fuck!" Randy was already gulping down deep breaths of air, burning his lungs as he looked around wildly, trying to catch his bearings. He didn't know how he had made it this far, but his feet carried him further down grated flooring, past remnants of forgotten construction, chalked letters that reminded him more of satanic pentagrams than numbers and lines meant for measurements and grading.

The thought didn't last long.

Like a thunderous crack of movement and shadow they appeared. The tremble felt beneath his feet was only the beginning, as a demonic predator suddenly stood before him and one behind, two flanking from the left and right, boxing him in. Licking their lips. Obviously faster than the others of this supernatural hell.

Conroy could already see the other demonic beasts catching up. Phantoms and wraiths, shadowed and blurred; stalking down bulkheads like living gargoyles and hanging from catwalks like grinning devils, waiting for the pounce. For that new soul to be had.

He could hear the devil's words whispering in the back of his mind, words about how Randy was *trapped*, no matter how far he ran.

A prison of bone and flesh.

A brethren in the hundreds following the unspoken order of a devil dreaming of the end.

The finality of everything.

The banality of evil, my ass! Conroy stood his ground.

And that was when Randy thought he heard rain coming down heavy on metal. But it wasn't water.

No, it wasn't rain...

It was blood.

His blood.

CHAPTER FORTY-ONE

Blood & Steel

The realization hit him like a shockwave.

He was bleeding.

Badly.

His flesh was torn away from his arm. Four deep, jagged gouges. Conroy still felt the claws on his skin, as if those sharpened tools were still locked tight, the way an amputee feels a phantom limb. He shivered at the thought.

The idea of the claws swiping again at his throat or his face, his abdomen or...or lower.

But it wasn't going to happen, not *yet*. No, he would make them *work* for his soul.

Conroy propelled himself forward with all of his might, again going for the default moves he used when in the ring at Grillo's. He was lightheaded and pale, and he knew damn well that the coppery smell in the air was blood.

That didn't bother him. The fact that it was *his* blood, well, *that* was a different story.

In addition, his rational mind--fighting to keep on track in an un-rational situation--told him that he was being tracked by the scent. It wouldn't be long now. The demons had let him flee, because they were predators. And, grimly, he came to the assumption that they had to build up their appetite.

He was barely able to make it past a seventh step when his legs grew weak, yet still they pumped and kicked, as he charged over the grated flooring. Puddles of mud splashed up around his ankles, mixed with oil and rust. Conroy could no longer hear the noise from above, any sounds of human life were now long gone.

The ship gently moving, the unseen lights of Long Beach glowing in the distance beyond this steel.

Passengers and crew members back in their rooms or offices, safe in their beds, behind locked doors. In the case of the former, a full belly of hot supper, perhaps followed by a few cocktails, lulling them into quiet and content comfort zones.

Dream well, live long happy lives.

Because Randy Conroy was nearing the finality of his own.

CHAPTER FORTY-TWO

Ashes to Ashes

Suddenly, two separate entities appeared in front of him. Conroy quickly aimed his flashlight's beam at their torsos a split-second later, the result causing their cries to resound through the massive belly of the Queen Mary, as the bright light burned at their forms.

The air around Randy had become a whirlwind of razor sharp teeth snapping, alternating with talons that whipped back and forth, raking at the light and his flesh. What appeared to be hind legs looked as if they could easily crush his weak bones into powder, and those amber eyes that he met with his own, ohhh they burned with bloodlust.

Those beasts were massive, with arched backs and front legs that were primed to rip into their next victim. And they behaved like a pack, but it was something else, something...*more*. A hive mind, a collective subconscious. Yet still a unit of singularity, each creature with its own specific purpose.

The smaller of the damned were drawing attention away from the larger, drawing Randy's attention as the others moved in for the kill. Their thoughts were known, shared; these demonic entities, driven by poltergeist activity were relentless.

Their skin was hairless, the color of ash, pulled and stretched against muscle like drum skin, but ripped and torn down to reddish-brown sinew in patches. Spinal columns that protruded razor sharp, reaching from the lowest arch of their backs to the crown of their foreheads. Conroy thought of pages from a notebook, a folder falling and fanning open like a "V". That is what the creatures' spines looked like, rising vile-colored for several inches, thinning to a pale white line, hopelessly sharp.

In truth, what they were could not be described in words: their faces a terrible haunting mix, yet wisdom and ancient creation, an ancient birth of the soulless and damned lived their, as well. Yes, they were born of Hell, born of a creator, an *artist* of flesh and despair beyond the black, and Conroy could not fathom that, only days ago, he was attending his grandfather's funeral on a chilled Minnesota morning.

The monsters tore through the ship like a hurricane through a grass hut, attacking Conroy as if he had trespassed within their own sanctuary. Where others would have pleaded with hands held high, clutching the reliquaries of their faith to no avail, he instead stood his ground, fighting with every breath drawn.

Other men would have begged and screamed for these creatures to spare their lives, pleading to anyone with the power, weapons, or faith to cast out the demons that now clawed around Randy.

Yet *he* fought on.

He was not braver nor stronger than the rest of humanity, he was just simply...*tired*. Blood-loss, exhaustion, beaten and torn. The darkness drank of

159

his life, had worn him down and had taken bits and pieces of his flesh.

So be it.

If this was to be his last stand, he would be damned--even more so--if he did not try to take some of their own with him. And so he ran. And so he fought.

Ashes to ashes, dust to dust.

The darkness ripped through walls of rivets and steel as if they were nothing but cardboard. Certainly, they would have butchered and eaten any other soul before they had a chance to react accordingly, by screaming or raising a weapon in defense, but instead, the darkness screamed...

And rightly so.

The air pressure dropped, Conroy wasn't certain if his ears had popped or if everything had suddenly turned louder. He felt a murderous heat, something no mortal man was ever meant to truly know. He, like humanity, like *man*, was still far too young to unlock such things, such *sights*.

This...was where dead men walked.

And *this*, was where HE stood. Mr. Thetepet, the devil clapping his hands together in wicked enjoyment, laughing at the torment of the young man wrapped in nightmares.

The devil's speed was beyond inhuman, his movement entirely animalistic, a complete predator. He dispatched the ghostly presence pursuing Conroy within mere seconds, the devil's eyes focused with intent, the scent of his prey in the air. Sweet and reeking of fear. It was rapture and passion.

The thought that Conroy's soul belonged to him.

Randy's flashlight was dimming, the batteries running low, but if he focused well enough, he could still discern the smallest of shadows. The echoing concussion of his footsteps on the grating was deafening in the enclosed space as he charged forward. The devil was leaping from wall to wall, his top hat never once slipping from his head.

The devil too was avoiding the light, and the pack of creatures were at his side, ground level. A brethren. A dark family.

They had torn throughout the ship in a matter of minutes in pursuit of the damned, they knew the layout of this vessel by heart, and the dead were all accounted for. Nothing had mattered but their master's mission. Nothing mattered but their success. Their cries were heard as a screeching roar of Hell...

...seen upon the blood splattered walls of this damned tourist attraction.

And only the shortest of distances separated them from their prize, from Conroy's strong, yet fragile, soul.

He couldn't comprehend why they were so hell-bent on surrounding him, but he understood that they needed him alive. This despite the torn flesh of his arm, the blood trailing in rivulets. But he would not waver, because devil or not, the man in the top hat had answers. The key to the puzzle box wrapped in the decomposing flesh and bones of his grandfather.

A reason for it all.

Conroy had an epiphany, it came from being lightheaded, and he quickly unthreaded his brown leather belt with one huge tug, and a cracking snap echoed down the empty corridors. He saw this in an old film he had seen back in high school, along with how to perform CPR and other lifesaving techniques. And shit, if it worked for John McClane, then *yippie-ki-yay*.

Once the belt was wrapped around his shredded arm, he pulled tight enough to feel the pressure in his toes. He fought through the pain. Pushed himself harder than he had ever done before. He fought as he would at Grillo's, focused mentally as if he were working on a *deadline*. Pun intended.

He had the flashlight tucked in his pants pocket while he secured the belt and then just like that, it was once more in hand, a few droplets of blood smearing the light. He felt an ache in his side and he knew that behind him the demonic creatures gave chase, he knew from the sounds of devastation echoing past him that they never stopped.

And then, the worst possible thing occurred. If Randy hadn't turned back to look at the demons giving pursuit, he would likely have dodged the low hanging beam, because he would have been in a crouch. Instead his forehead cracked against the unforgiving steel, and his blood spattered flashlight went spinning from his hands like a giant Fourth of July sparkler.

Everything was a thin tunnel of sound and light. The light turned to blackness, a dark that was as constricting as the creatures' bloodlusts. Visions flipped through his mind like photos in a viewfinder. The ship during construction, during the war, dead, dead, and more dead, then suddenly the screaming.

His vision swam from blood loss, dark, like drifting below the surface of the water.

And that screaming, echoing around him.

They were HIS *screams.*

Then, the light. Everything had happened in split seconds, because he saw his flashlight still spinning, momentarily blinding him. Then, movement! From the corner of his eye he saw something, and he realized that the shadows were everywhere now. He could have laughed through his delirium at the absurdity of it all.

Seconds bled into moments and moments bled into--

bled

bleed.

Bleeding, the thought hitting Conroy's brain, three syllables, *I'm bleeding* and then the ground rushed up at him in an embrace of rust and oil as he bounced down the grating, past signs that read *Caution* and *Keep Out*, he was like a huge stone skipping over water.

His vision, his thoughts fading fast. Everything spinning, blurred. Everything dark...

The world smelled like death to Randy, now motionless, his face buried in the Queen Mary's steel.

Yes, *everything* was dark.

Dark...as in death.

CHAPTER FORTY-THREE

Dust to Dust

Conroy tried to stand, realizing with sudden clarity where he was, and that he needed to get the hell out of there. *Desperately* so, in fact. As fast as humanly possible.

He realized now that it had been a bad idea to venture this far with only a Mag-Lite and the strength in his soul. A bad idea to believe that he alone could end this.

To be so proud to not ask for help.

He was hanging halfway over the ledge, with the massive, sliding steel door twisted several feet behind him. Like a discarded aluminum can of obscene proportions. *Yes*, he thought with sarcasm, he had indeed arrived, because he was hanging halfway over a ledge that would drop him into that deep, dark pit where, in another time, German prisoners of war had been crammed together.

The place where Mr. Thetepet--The Tempter-- was once imprisoned.

Conroy was in the devil's home. Far below any human habitation, as deep within the Queen Mary as possible.

He was now within her womb.

And her womb was the devil's playground.

"*All alone*," The Tempter growled. A sound somewhere between man and beast, yet filled with sorrow and pain. "*In the ennnnd, you're alllwayysss byyy yourrsssselfff. You're allll you've got. Family, materialisssstic treasssuress,* fressshhhh and newwww *lovessss.*" The voice was sibilant, hypnotic, echoing. He motioned as if something was beside Conroy. Something chilling.

He looked and saw nothing, then turned back to Mr. Thetepet and the devil was now cradling one of his demonic little children. Rocking it like it was some sort of fake doll.

"They are nothing." No more echoes, the voice deepening. "Because nothing remains in the end. Only the demons that haunt you. In *this* life, or the next."

"What are you?" Conroy asked, bluntly. "What do you want?"

Mr. Thetepet stood his ground, releasing the child. His gaze was lost in Conroy's own. Conroy could finally see that there was no life in the demon, that the thing before him had been an empty shell for a very long time.

And it became crystal clear to him that he was slowly being driven to suicide, just as his grandfather had been. Another soul to the call. Randy kicked himself away, a feeble attempt at protection, a *pathetic* attempt at survival.

"*What do you want!*" Conroy's voice was the sound of a gunshot.

"Can you hear it?" The devil smiled grimly.

"Hear what?" Conroy asked, fatigue in his voice.

And then, momentary silence, until the demon again smiled, a vicious hate in his eyes. A voice that was deep and direct. Cold.

"The drumbeats of war."

War? What the hell was it talking about?

165

As he thought those words, the devil was suddenly beside him.

"The suffering here is...*exquisite*."

And then Conroy tried to stand, he tried, desperately so, to push himself away from the edge, but a blinding blow to the back of his head caused all of the veins in his eyes to expand and his retinas dilated as he fell to the floor once more.

The back of his head was in such pain, his ears still ringing. He could feel..."wet" trailing down his neck. He struggled to shake off the disorientation. Something had struck him, and it was the hardest blow he had ever felt. But, wait. It wasn't the ringing in his ears that he heard. No, not at all, it was a word, slowly forming and connecting, a puzzle of sound piecing together, until he could hear that single word clearly.

"MINE!""

Such a simple word.

And with it, he was kicked over the edge into spinning darkness.

CHAPTER FORTY-FOUR

The Fall

The demonic predators stopped no more than a hair's breadth from their human feast.

Which was Conroy, of course.

There was no denying the barely restrained tempest of rage within their inhuman eyes. Yet they held back.

Conroy groped at the dark pit he was in, and as soon as he reached out, every nerve ending and muscle in his back screamed out with vicious assault. His pain was excruciating. He had fallen too far downward, the echoes and cries of those long damned and doomed Nazis made him clap his hands over his ears. *More* pain.

He might have been drawing breath, may have still been able to walk, but he was very much in hell.

Looking around, he saw that the darkness had taken him into another nightmare, another dimension.

Another reality.

Christ, maybe he was trapped inside his own tormented mind! He knew this wasn't real, this new place he had found himself within. He knew that he was still in the dark steel hold, but the fact didn't stop him from clawing at the muddy earth, ripping out clumps of grass which oozed between his fingers as he felt himself being pulled back. Claws

167

held his legs firmly in place. Pain made it a certainty.

He wouldn't be going anywhere.

Randy knew there was no escape. He had become his grandfather. And he knew with complete certainty that the muddy earth beneath him would become his tomb. Real or not, that black and brown mud and slime covered him over like quicksand, effectively encasing him in a liquid crypt, a grimace on his face and clawing fingers simply frozen forever.

Would he just be left there, in tatters? Broken and bruised, devoured in mind, body, and soul...blood long dried upon the cold steel while revelers danced and dined hundreds of feet above his corpse for those many, *many* years to come?

Was *this* his fate?

Or was it simply *the beginning*?

Randy looked overhead, expecting to see the riveted ceiling, but instead saw demonic-vultures circling high above him; the shriveled, stillborn bodies of the lost fused to their black-feathered bellies. Their wailing cries echoing beyond this scorched earth. And across the distance, Abigail, his only love, his *true* love, screaming without sound.

Screaming...for *him*.

Without thought, without fail, he raced toward her. And he did not falter. He did not fail. Nothing held him at bay. He had to save her. He *would* save her.

As he approached, drawing closer with each aching muscle, fueled by adrenaline alone, he skidded to a shocking, mind-numbing halt as he saw more of the Nazi dead. Gory visages, flesh ripped away from the jaws and necks, teeth chattering in demonic glory. No longer human, something born of the deepest reaches of Hell's creations.

Conroy spun through the shock as the Germans began beating on him. Tongue-less mouths shouting orders in their native language. He tried to fight back, using skills he knew by heart, and he could hear a younger Grillo berating him for every misstep.

But it was futile. His body was beaten down. One after another, the undead Nazis struck him further down, down towards the scorched earth, down toward what lie BEYOND Hell. No longer muddy, but cracked and desolate.

His eyes never left Abigail's gaze as she looked on helplessly. Tears streamed down her beautiful face. In that face he saw love and pain, but he also saw regret.

Drops of his blood spattered on the dry ground. Barbed wire curled upward from where the crimson drops nourished the earth. His body was not only beaten and cracked, it was brutalized by these Nazi beasts...and they laughed as one at his torment.

And then, two polished black boots passed him by. Seizing his will, Conroy screamed out his rage, but it wasn't real. No, his mind was cracking. Splitting into two grey masses. He was pleading with Abigail to run, he screamed with every ounce of oxygen left within his lungs, as his body once more felt the brutal impact of demonic strength.

The head demon, the Nazi with the shit-shined boots, approached Abigail. It's skinless smile was large and frightening, and it reached toward her,

169

taking her chin and pushing her face so that she had no choice but to see Conroy through widened eyes.

"Please...run..." The words rasped from Randy's throat.

But she remained silent, even as the Nazis made him dig a hole. He dug into the black earth, it was as hard as the steel he had left behind for this new world. But, no...he was *on* the ship, and his bare hands were what he used to shovel the dirt.

His nails tore away, one by one, as he dug at the Queen Mary's hull. This was his life now, a prison of bone and flesh. And that was when he heard the music.

Carnival music.

A demonic carny wearing a fedora and jauntily swinging a cane passed along with his carnival of horrors behind him. Performing for the Nazis as Conroy continued digging.

"Dig! Dig!" The carny screamed. "Dig hard, dig deep! Digging through what we reap! Come one, come all, look at the man who took the *fall*!"

A crowd of onlookers had gathered, watching Conroy, he heard one say to another the words 'new meat' as he nodded towards the piled dirt. Deformed fathers carried equally disfigured sons on their shoulders. A cotton candy roll replaced by a cotton candy stick of eyes. Clowns, no different than the ones one would see at a carnival in the real world, performed various acts as the deformed brats squealed in delight and awe.

They were all there, tributes to the classic Bearded Lady, Strong Man, the Fire Eater and the Lizard Boy, the Tallest Man, a psychic and conjoined twins were performing their own freak show. Alive with hideous delight, nightmare interpretations, far worse inside the Queen Mary than what they might have been in the outside world. In that *real* world.

And as the last of them passed, Randy had finished digging.

Crawling out from the trench, he saw that Abigail was released, her delicate feet never touching the scorched earth. She was floating across the expanse, as she brought her face close to his, kissing him passionately until he realized that it wasn't her.

It wasn't Abigail, it never had been.

Her kisses...didn't taste like death.

He tried to push back, but a mass of snakes had created THIS Abigail's body. *Medusa's bastard.* And they pushed back. HARDER.

"Together forever?" Hisses came from it's mouth as it pulled back the snakes that made up her face like bubble gum and pasta.

Chained angels were being led to an endless pit; their wings sheered clean and tossed over the edge to fall towards the fire forever. Conroy reeled back and fell into the shallow hole he had dug, into the maggot-riddled earth. And before he hit the ground dirt was being tossed on top of him.

An *inverted cross* planted into the earth.

And Randy was able to see it, as the last shovelful of mud spilled into his eyes.

CHAPTER FORTY-FIVE

The Devil's Playground

Randy was crying out, then screaming, gasping for air, for daylight and salvation.

But then...

Then he was back in the bowels of the ship, as he had been for hours. No hole had been dug, no demonic carnies mocking him in joyous celebration. It was all in his head, equal parts madness and the devil's design.

A playground of horrors.

He glanced around and realized that he had been digging at steel, and it was in that moment of realization, of *clarity*, that he knew one thing was certain...no matter if he made it out of this nightmare or not, he would be leaving his fingernails far behind. He would be leaving *bits and pieces* of his flesh and soul in this world of damnation.

The offering, the *Gospel of Conroy*, paid in full.

Paid...to HIM.

Beyond the massive frames of the demonic predators, there he was, the form of Mr. Thetepet taking shape. A darkened blob becoming a walking human-like form of existence.

The top hat and grin.

Conroy levered his body off the floor at the sight of the devil's approach, and almost choked on what had been churning in his stomach. He could feel bile forcing its way into his esophagus.

He groaned lazily, defiant to the end, as he looked the devil in the eyes, ignoring the fact that his vision was blurring from the loss of blood, and he couldn't discern if the hallucinations were a part of it or not.

Those eyes, the devil's eyes, looked directly into his own, and they were filled with an evil so palpable it projected ripples into its red irises like heartbeats of acid. They could have leaked, like the yoke of a broken egg into Conroy's own, blinding him.

It was a literal manifestation of hate, and *that* was why he thought he was hallucinating. But it was also a certainty that the red in the devil's eyes *was* dripping down its cheeks like burning trails, traces of mercury. With only black ichor remaining within the sockets.

Yes, he *was* crazy and none of this was happening. Sure. That had to be it. Why the hell not? His sanity had become as flawed as his grandfather's. Shattered like a mirror. Yes, he was in a padded cell somewhere, nice and comfy. Rocking back and forth in a wheelchair, wild stories in his head, drool past his lips. Shock therapy and curfew.

But he knew this wasn't the case, why was he aware of the darkness around him if it was, the place where the demons had brought him? Stale, fetid air, not the gentle breeze of a sanitarium's front lawn. And if he was that crazy, then why was Mr. Thetepet still there, smiling at him? Dressed in a

173

white lab coat now with a stethoscope decorating his neck?

More mysteries to be unlocked, more puzzle pieces of bone and flesh to solve, but first, Randy had to worry foremost about the fact that the beasts might yet be nearing for a final encore. He suspected that the shadows had no need to devour him *yet*, but they indeed started to drag him further into the darkness. Further from the light. From Abigail...

He couldn't question why, his throat was too raw. Regardless, their replies would have only been snarls of rage. Perhaps they would eat him in privacy, away from the eyes of the real world.

Conroy wanted to gather his voice long enough to ask if Mr. Thetepet was too much of a pussy to kill him himself. He wanted to be *defiant* to the end. And so he said nothing, forcing himself to remain calm in his final minutes. Or hours. *Whatever*.

Accept your fate, Randy. Go out like a man. Like Papa.

But as Mr. Thetepet knelt over him, like a demonic moral judge, that damn grin ever present, Conroy felt a searing pain in his chest, his back, then his forearms. The devil was reaching past sinew and muscle for his soul. Or at least it felt as if that was what was happening.

"My God," Conroy said, so simple, to the point. No more words were needed.

"God?" Mr. Thetepet replied through his grin. "No, no, no. Such a pity that you pray to *him*, such a pity...for God does not hear the sinners."

He wanted to be brave, but the devil was now devouring chunks of his flesh, so all he could do was scream.

"What do you want from me!" His voice echoing harshly as he bellowed with all his might. "What do you want! WHAT THE FUCK DO YOU WANT!

Mr. Thetepet couldn't help but smile wider with reply.

"Mine-mine-mine."

CHAPTER FORTY-SIX

"Ghosts & Legends" Attraction Entrance
"D" Deck, Wharf Tower, Elevator Level 1

After the fall...

Abigail paced back and forth across the cement floor. She knew Randy would have entered through these doors, because this was where the "Paranormal Ship Walk Tour" began. It was also the area where a tour was given to relate the story of War Brides during WWII. About the fitting of the anti-aircraft guns, the 70th anniversary of its maiden voyage, and more recent events. It was all history and sepia, captured in the gritty black & white of memory.

Where she stood, before these massive double doors--and God how they hadn't loomed so large before--was where the Queen Mary's storied history was left behind, to be replaced by that of the paranormal.

This is where it began; he had to have stepped through these doors. There was no other way. He didn't necessarily have to exit through them though, he could have easily exited through the First Class Swimming Pool area. That is, if he could find his way, as the ship truly was a maze, a nonlinear path of darkness and shadows. But it was something in her gut, something she felt all the way down to the marrow in her bones, something that told her he

176

would be back. That he would be released from whatever torments lie beyond.

He would come back into the light of day.

Through. These. Two. Doors.

Now, four (*or was it six?*) hours later, she wasn't so sure. That was how long she had waited, *hours*. Hours that felt like an eternity.

And then the doors exploded open...and the bloody mess that was Randy Conroy toppled through.

Abigail could only see the huge amounts of blood, hear his never-ending screams, and stare into his eyes that were permanently wide in fear and pain.

Gulping down air to the point of hyperventilation, he fell into her waiting arms and she pulled him close as his screams continued, screams that could wake the dead. It was the worst sound she had ever heard.

People gathered, hearing the commotion, and security personnel raced toward them. Somewhere in the distance, police and EMTs were dispatched. Conroy's body steamed with heat, yet it was cold to the touch. Like a dead body released from Hell.

He was on the same path that the angels were...the angels from that hellish nightmare of carnies and demonic Nazis. Yes, he was like the angels...forever falling, and sheered clean of all that made him whole.

Abigail was crying and screaming herself. *What had happened? My God, what had--*

And through his bloody screams, Randy Conroy could only mutter in monotone.

"GET ME OFF THIS SHIP!"

PART FOUR:
THERAPY

*"[A]s children tremble and fear everything
in the blind darkness, so we in the light
sometimes fear what is no more to be
feared than the things children in the dark
hold in terror..."*

--LUCRETIUS
On the Nature of Things
(ca. 60 B.C.)

CHAPTER FORTY-SEVEN

November 30, 2011. Bright Spell, Minnesota.
Psychiatric Office of Dr. Douglas Thorne.

4:15 PM

Dr. Thorne sat behind his desk in a comfortable manner, much as he did every day, handling the middling concerns of the neighboring population and their "mental health" *issues*. Mental health issues that were easily solved by prescribing sleeping pills, suggesting a different diet, or simply listening to the ailments and anguishes that were almost always a reflection of bad daytime television.

But this time, little more than five weeks having passed since he had first met Randy Conroy, Thorne believed his assessment was wrong. Whatever psychological break that had claimed the elder Conroy's sanity had now taken root and burrowed deep into the young man's subconsciousness.

Randy Conroy was *becoming* his grandfather...

"So you believe in the paranormal," Thorne began as the wall clock ticked into the session's first minute.

"Yes," Conroy said, shifting on the couch. "I believe."

"What exactly do you believe in, Mr. Conroy?"

"The kind of *things* you don't." Using emphasis.

"Well," Thorne said, "that is indeed quite the story..."

Conroy stared at the psychiatrist, their eyes were level. "I'm aware."

"Why do you think it is this...Mr. Thetepet, this man--"

"It's not a man," Conroy interrupted.

"No, of course not," Thorne placated his client. "Just a figure of speech, mind you. Again, why do you think this Mr. Thetepet, this individual you believe to be the devil, just... let you go?"

"I don't know," Conroy said. "I went down into that darkness to try and understand and...and to put an end to all of this. I didn't know how I was going to do it, but..." He shifted in his seat again. "I had to put an end to it somehow. What had happened to my grandfather, what appeared to be happening to me, as well. But--"

Randy stopped, ready to cry. But he held the tears at bay. He fought, not with fists, but with heart.

"I don't know why it let me go." He spoke faster now, letting the words fight the emotion. "I don't know why it didn't, I don't know, *explain* something, *anything* to me. I mean, what was the purpose for all of this? Why lead me to the ship and then..."

Just the clock ticked now, silence and time. Nothing more. And when that "silence" became deafening--

"Mr. Conroy?"

Randy looked up. He looked up and could only whisper with whatever was left of him. "There was no rhyme nor reason when I looked into its eyes."

He paused.

182

"There was no *purpose* other than enjoyment. It was...*enjoying* itself."

"But you went down there to confront it in some way?"

"To find answers," Randy said, more to the point. "Yes."

"And other than these horrific events, as you've described them, did you find such answers?"

"No," Randy looked at the floor. "I found nothing. Just more questions. The ship just attacked, and then after a few hours of hell, it simply...it simply let me go."

"The *ship* itself attacked?" Thorne leaned in. "You mean you were lost and found yourself in a decrepit portion of the vessel? You mean wood and beams, possibly loose from age, had fallen on you? Bruises, scrapes, things like that?"

"No. *The actual ship* attacked me." He knew how it sounded, but Thorne nodded to himself and scrawled notes into his journal.

"Okay. This young woman, Abigail Marshall, she witnessed these events, as well?"

"No," Conroy answered. "Like I said, I went down there alone. To protect her."

"Right, right." Saying it like this was all news to him. "But she's staying with you now? At your grandmother's house while you--"

"While I figure out a way to end this. To stop whatever it is that's haunting the Queen Mary, because that in itself is what haunted my grandfather. What had driven him to suicide."

"But, Mr. Conroy," Thorne said, putting his pen back on the desk. "You haven't experienced any of these, I don't know...hauntings, any paranormal activity since you've arrived back home. That's what you told me...so if it's *haunting* the Queen Mary than how can it haunt *you* at home?"

"This isn't my home," Randy said. "I live in New York. I'm just visiting here, I'm trying to--"

"I understand," Thorne said calmly. "You're trying to stop this darkness, it is all right here in my notes."

"I'm not crazy," Randy's hands clenched the sides of the couch. "My grandfather *wasn't* crazy!"

"Calm down, Mr. Conroy, I'm just trying to better understand."

Dr. Thorne once again took up pen in hand and wrote down a few more lines in his notebook, then continued.

"Answer me this, Mr. Conroy. Why are you still trying to understand these mysteries, as you call them, to stop this darkness within the Queen Mary, if it appears you've been, well...released?"

"Just because I haven't experienced anything in a few days, maybe a week--"

"*Weeks*, Mr. Conroy. It's been weeks."

"You know what I meant. Just because I haven't experienced anything since I got off that ship, doesn't mean its over." Conroy's voice rose. "If it doesn't come back for me, it will just come back for somebody else. If this *thing* isn't stopped and destroyed, if it *can't* be stopped and destroyed, at least people can be warned. They *need* to be warned."

"You mean like your grandfather tried to warn people?"

"I'm not my gran--I'm not like my grandfather."

"No. I suppose not...So, Ms. Marshall is your girlfriend?" Thorne asked pointedly.

"Abigail is helping me with research," Randy said. "She's helping me find a way, she's, look, I've told you all of this already." His tone turned towards one of impatience.

"Okay, then," Thorne said, still using the same calming tone. "So now you believe in the hauntings of the Queen Mary. And when we first spoke, after the funeral, before you had left town, you believed your grandfather had been ill and his stories were nothing more than fiction, delusions of a broken mind."

Conroy nodded once.

"And now, you believe differently," Thorne looked right at Conroy. "Now you unequivocally know that ghosts exist."

To which Conroy nodded once more.

"And do you have any proof of your so-called discovery?" Thorne leaned back, not meaning to look pompous.

"You don't believe me." A flat statement.

"Mr. Conroy, I really am just like you," Thorne said. "Trying to unlock the mystery of what is going on within your mind."

The volley went back and forth, Conroy saying how Thorne must think him crazy with a chemical imbalance, or worse. Thorne then countered that Conroy's problems manifested *after* his grandfather's death.

The worst possible thing to suggest.

Conroy stood apprehensively, then tore at his overshirt, ripping several buttons off in the process. A now torn flannel hiding the same secret that his grandfather did. The same nightmare. It was a tapestry of sin upon his canvas of flesh. For he too was branded by the devil. It was the same symbol he had seen in that faded photograph in what seemed like a lifetime ago.

An intricate detail of carved flesh. Claw, tooth, talon...whatever inhuman tool it was, had carved what could only be described as the torments of hell. The rings, the circles, the pit...it was ALL apparent. And right there, front and center, was his grandfather's visage, among the rest of the damned.

"You know what it whispered in my ear before it did this to me?"

Thorne stood, backing away from the sight.

"Go ahead and give me the beast...you already have my hate."

CHAPTER FORTY-EIGHT

Elder Conroy Residence, Mound, Minnesota.

Randy and Abigail were staying alone in what was now his grandmother's house. A widow who couldn't bear to be reminded of her late husband and was staying with one of her younger sisters. Away from the prying eyes, away from the whispers. Away from all that pity. Apparently the two old gals spent most of their time grieving at one of the Indian casinos, the Mystic or...or something like that, so Conroy really couldn't understand where her grief truly lie.

But for Randy and Abigail, here in this place, they often sat in silence, trying to figure out how to end the nightmare that they still believed was confined to the Queen Mary. The only *logical* explanation.

Logical...yeah.

Ignorance is bliss.

†††††

Later on that night, after arriving home from Thorne's office and another trip to the library for more research materials, they had dinner and made love. They both agreed to forego any research until later on, and spent some time sitting by a window overlooking a snowy field, wrapped in one another's

187

arms. Soft kisses. Lingering looks. They almost felt...normal.

Abigail set the timer on her camera and the end result was a photograph of the two of them locked together forever in the perfect kiss.

Forever. That was the plan.

Then, still sitting intimately, she asked Randy how the trip to the therapist went, treading ever so lightly. She remembered his anger and frustration upon their arrival at his grandmother's house. Nothing but a note to greet them about a casserole in the fridge and hopes of a royal flush. *With love,* the young Conroy thought, *the bitch who didn't care if the corpse was cold yet or not...*Soon after, Randy had begun to spend increasing amounts of time in his grandfather's den. Still trying to unlock the mysteries behind the evil that haunted his dreams.

His notes and research, the books on hauntings and poltergeist activities, from ancient texts delving into the darkness of Hell to the equally cryptic quotations in the Old Testament filled his every waking moment.

Still on his quest, so close to unlocking the mysteries, but, as was the case with his grandfather, he was missing that one crucial piece of the puzzle.

The answer to "Why?"

All of the research, the results, compiled and compartmentalized in his laptop. As the psychiatrist had said, his search for knowledge was an affliction. Around and around he went.

Can you hear it?

The devil in the top hat, grinning as he whispered to Conroy. The hisses echoed and haunted his memories.

Can you hear it?

Yes, like the fingernails of ghosts against broken glass.

Can you hear it?

Like claw and teeth digging through brain matter with ease.

Can you hear THE DRUMBEATS OF WAR?

Yes, he thought. *I can hear it. God help us all, I can hear it.*

It *was* a war, one being fought for his sanity. And for his very soul.

Forcing out the blur of horror and carnage from his mind, Conroy looked at the world that lay in ruin around him. A grim sight matching the grim expression on his face. What had his world become? And now, with Abigail, what did *their* future hold?

Nothing made sense anymore.

Nothing but death.

CHAPTER FORTY-NINE

December 1, 2011.
3:00 AM

The Devils Hour

Four hours had passed, with Conroy asleep at his grandfather's desk in a sea of untidy calm. For all intents and purposes, this was *still* his grandfather's home. His *sanctuary*.

It was here that his grandfather had relaxed by supping single malt whiskey while listening to the classics. Jazz, blues, a little Sidney Bechet, a little Ray Charles, all depending on the mood. That's why it wasn't the same this early morning of a devil's hour, it would *never* be the same. This wasn't a consecrated place to Conroy, this was a means to an end.

And he certainly wasn't relaxed at all, not even when sleep took him. A war was coming and there was a voice in his dreams, a whisper ever so calm which called out to his inner soul.

A whisper beckoning.

A whisper in the cries.

Around Conroy's slumped form, head tilted to the right in troubled sleep, were a dozen opened books. Pages on spiritualism and paranormal images and photographs, and on top of those lay research papers, piled on every available surface. To the right, the framed photograph of his grandfather, so

190

very different than he once remembered, was placed face down.

Happier times better left in the past, better left in the dark where they belonged. Like the voice.

Conroy's grandfather had destroyed himself, his marriage, his very life; it was just like a macabre story when he chose that path years past. He had noosed the devil and watched him hang. It was a ripple effect that would tear through his own life and devour the lives of all those he held dear.

And Randy too had made his own bed, and, like his grandfather, he would have to lie in it.

††††††

His neck was stiff, a pinched nerve certainly awaited him, when the ancient texts of biblical lore suddenly began to darken. It was as if all light, all warmth, was being sucked out of the room. Like lost souls coming to reclaim their forgotten lives in a den torn apart due to the many hours of research.

A singing distortion of pain and sorrow, like crystals in a cavernous grotto echoing their lullaby. Conroy wasn't awakened by the cold or the dark, it was the voice in his darkened dreams.

Mr. Thetepet.

The Tempter.

Only through sacrifice comes redemption.

And then the chair kicked back out from under him and Conroy was suddenly standing erect, pinpricks of light stabbed into his clouded eyes. His fists were clenched into tight balls, the shock and disorientation of being forced awake lingered as he awaited what the mysterious form, backlit by the light, had in store for him.

"No," Conroy tried to sound determined, but that uncertain fog still clouded his vision. And then again. "*No.*"

He wasn't on the Queen Mary, he was hundreds of miles north and east, it couldn't be there because it was confined to the ship.

It was a *part* of the ship.

It was CONFINED TO THE SHIP!

Turned out...it wasn't.

The figure began moving, cautious and alert, a hunter circling his prey. Each movement precisely measured. A half circle to the left, half again to the right, always keeping Conroy at arm's length, close enough to claim, but far enough away to keep him at ease.

And then the devil spoke, stepping into the dimly lit world that was the elder Conroy's home.

"*Weeee miisssss yoouu.*"

"*What do you want from me?*" Conroy demanded, turning slowly, the same question asked over and over, again and again in his nightmares, as he fixed the devil with an unfaltering glare. "Answer me! Answer me, damn you!"

The devil said only one word. "YOU."

And Conroy knew that the devil would have his due.

CHAPTER FIFTY

The Devils Hour
&
Later still...

They were alone for the night and Abigail was going to take Randy away from the horrific thoughts that swarmed in his head. She would take him away from the shared horrors they had seen on the Queen Mary. She would chase away his fears.

It seemed much longer than a mere month ago, *was that right*? *FOUR WEEKS WITHOUT INCIDENT*, she'd think in a joking manner. Yet she knew she wouldn't be laughing if she had seen what her love had seen, in truth her need to make light of the matter masked the inward terror she herself had felt that night.

And *every* night since...

So it was as much for her emotional needs as it was for Randy.

Even if she knew that she was lying to herself.

There was a sense of normalcy, but one had to know how to make things right. Abigail had brought things from Long Beach to Randy's grandparents' house, those certain things she sought out in times of comfort. Her way of escape...

A powder blue blanket with ivory colored stripe her mother had crocheted. A few of her favorite movies and books to lose herself within. Music.

Always music. And a big ol' stereo system to drown out the world.

And so the volume was cranked up, the lead singer of LADY, THAT'S MY SKULL's throaty voice wailed away on the eleventh track like an exorcism gone horribly wrong. The band had been together for decades, pre-grunge and post-glam back in California, and each group member looked like they'd just graduated from high school. The echoing base line thumped, the guitar riffs charged, and the beat of the drums made Abigail's voice vibrate to the accompanied lyrics. She sang and danced like there was no tomorrow. Here, in this house, with *her* Randy Conroy, she felt...she felt that rarity of freedom.

And because of that, she almost didn't hear him.

"GET OUT OF THE HOUSE!" Randy yelled as loud as he could.

She turned, momentarily surprised that it sounded like he was *right* behind her. His voice was familiar, yet hauntingly different. Like it was tainted, *infected*.

Infected with pure hate.

"Randy?" Abigail wanted to touch him. "Baby, what's wrong?" Yes...she wanted to chase it all away.

And yet fear dripped from each syllable, and she began a slow stride of uncertainty, as her nerves desperately fought to calm down in the seconds after the outburst.

She took another step toward the staircase leading to the den, but stopped because she saw the look on her lover's face at the top of the stairs. A look she'd never forget as he slowly backed out of

194

the room...as he turned and looked at what was standing behind *her*.

His look. THAT look...it was a thing of horror.

"It's too late," Randy said. "Don't move."

He was terrified, and Abigail could only imagine what he was seeing.

She had to look, had to know, she just *had to*.

"Abigail, don't!" Randy almost screamed. "Close your eyes, baby. Close them tight."

But it was already too late. Some things you just...some things you just *can't* un-see.

Crouched before them was a nightmare born from some other place and time, born from one hell of a fucked up imagination. The creature was anthropomorphic in form, that much was certain, but it most resembled a lamprey. Jawless with a funnel-like sucking hole for a mouth, ringed by sharp teeth. Clawed fingers attached to gangly arms, and a short stalk of legs and padded feet. Chains hung from its elongated form and dripped with bile and saliva. It was branded by The Tempter.

Dimensions, realities, planets...Heaven or Hell, whatever it was, wherever it came from, only one thing was truly certain this night...*it was hungry*. And its mouth made horrible gurgling sounds as it tried to lick its nonexistent lips at the sight of Abigail.

All it saw...was Abigail.

"RUN!" Randy yelled.

It was that *same* hauntingly familiar voice that she had heard come from Randy's mouth, and Abigail didn't need to be told twice, but her legs wouldn't move.

Terror had her, and held her tight.

Conroy fought against every fear and uncertainty that wrapped itself around his spine and gnawed at his sanity as he flew down the stairs and took Abigail's hand in his own and ran.

He ran like the devil himself was giving chase. *Who knows*, he thought grimly. *Maybe another one was.*

CHAPTER FIFTY-ONE

By The Skin & The Teeth...

Conroy was fast, but the creature was faster.

He kicked at the beast snapping at his heels, and they all turned into the far corner in the maze of hallways that was his grandfather's house. Everything was moving too terribly quick, it was as if he and Abigail had suddenly found themselves swept into a hurricane of terror. *Another nightmare of Hell*. Different location, same players. It was just too difficult for him to comprehend, to think and process not only the situation, but the appearance and subtle movements of such a thing.

But what he *did* know, was that this wasn't a hunt. No...this was a game of cat and mouse. Abigail was screaming to the point of making herself sick, and Randy could tell that she was afraid to look back, yet unable to resist.

The hunter. The hunted. A thing from Hell coming for two human prey. Two human prey desperately trying to escape and evade the darkness in pursuit. Nothing but titles, *truths* and descriptions...It didn't matter really; it wasn't even a factor in this nightmare. No, this was becoming a mindless foot chase: immediate, frantic, and frightening. Titles or truths didn't matter in the nightmare, nor did the creature. Randy knew now that there would *always* be more nightmares around the next corner. This...this was simply something that would have once been born of his own active imagination, but after the events of the Queen Mary, the simple truth was: *this* was his life now.

This was home.

And the two of them ran while a new weapon of the devil pursued. One moment it was Abigail and Randy, and a moment later--three frames in a spool of film--a funnel of sharp teeth snapping, horrid limbs pumping. Down one hall, then left through the kitchen, the opposite hall bringing them back into the living room again. He could feel the testosterone and sweat in the air, every living person or thing in sheer overdrive. He never once looked back.

Compared to the incidents on the Queen Mary, this was undiluted *Hell*, through and through. Because now *Abigail* was in the devil's sights. Because now Abigail was in the home of the damned...home of Randy Conroy.

He was already through the living room and passing the laundry room, all he could see were piles of dark and light clothing in an abstract way, when he felt the creature on his back. Claws tearing into his shoulder.

Haven't I given enough, he thought weakly.

Randy cried out in pain, as the razor teeth made a separate set of grooves in his skin, and it was all he could do to push Abigail into a pile of towels before he started fighting against the creature that had begun climbing upon his shoulders.

Thing was, it didn't want Conroy. Dessert came first, as ordered by the devil. The creature shoved him aside, eyes fixated on the tasty prize, and it was then and only then that Abigail suddenly realized what "dessert" looked like.

198

You could keep calling it a different name, creature or demon, beast or monster, but regardless, it bolted forward.

At least, it seemed to.

With the exception of its gangly arms waving frantically toward Abigail, it wasn't moving forward, because Randy held tight to its legs. He held tight for *four*. *Long*. *Seconds*, as the creature turned back and stared at him with *malevolent* eyes.

And then Randy's fingers slipped. And then his hold...failed.

The creature was in the air in less than a heartbeat, a snarling ferocity coming down directly at Abigail, the dessert before the meal. She tried to shield herself and screamed in mind-numbing fright.

But then it was Randy joining in, *his* screams much louder, even as Abigail's diminished to hoarseness.

Randy could only watch as the demon clawed at Abigail's once beautiful face.

He could only watch...as the devil grinned.

CHAPTER FIFTY-TWO

It didn't matter...

Once, it had seemed like weeks. A handful of days. But no, no it had been longer.

Conroy was again walking listlessly to the therapist's office, months having passed since the hauntings born of that ancient darkness had followed both he and Abigail to New York. Yes, he had been back to Manhattan, but he couldn't really say for how long.

Had there been a Christmas tree in Rockefeller Center?

Was it a spring break for the damned?

It didn't matter--he had said, and thought it, a lot lately--*none of it mattered*. Because he had returned to Minnesota alone.

Abigail was no longer with him. And so he walked, not caring if it was sunny or cloudy, arid or humid. It just *didn't matter...*

He dwelled on that last night instead. The night that Mr. Thetepet's creature had chased them throughout his grandparents' house, stopping only after clawing at Abigail's face before retreating back into the darkness.

Half of Abigail's face had been ravaged so terribly that it could no longer be considered flesh, just a mess of jagged lines. One side still stunning and beautiful, the other distorted and destroyed.

Hideous.

It had been a lesson that the devil wanted Randy to learn. There would be *no way* to end this, no surgeries to *restore it*. He wasn't safe. SHE wasn't safe.

No one was.

They had been in New York for a little over a day before they went to see Grillo.

Conroy, walking through the ridiculously long parking lot towards the therapist's office, could only grimace as he thought of Jimmy, his best friend. His mentor. His pal.

Past tense.

Jimmy Grillo had suffered a massive coronary during their visit, screaming before the air escaped his lungs that there was something in the room with them, a man in a top hat with a hateful grin. And then he died. Just like that.

Randy then sent Abigail away, it was better to keep her in hiding. By separating, Mr. Thetepet could only concentrate on him. And so be it. They had made love one last time, and he left while she slept. Leaving a note that told her of his love for her, that it was better if she not see the ending to this confrontation, because there WOULD be an ending. One way or another.

Because the darkness was only truly after him, the direct bloodline to his grandfather. It pulled him from his bed at night, fires would suddenly spark in the kitchen, windows would shatter. Flames and glass forming words in a dead language, swirling in air and spelled out in jagged shapes on the floor. Demonic hatred raging forth.

He would awaken to missing items or shadowed forms, the poltergeist activity growing more violent by the day. Randy was no longer trying to unlock the mysteries behind his grandfather's suicide, he was attempting to puzzle out the mysteries of his own survival.

He may have been off the ship, as he had thought at some undetermined time in the past, but the ship did not let him go.

And it never would.

...So be it...

CHAPTER FIFTY-THREE

August 14, 2012. St. Paul, Minnesota.
Psychiatric Office of Dr. Michael Bailey.

5:45 PM

Conroy knew it was late summer, but he didn't care anymore. It was just like anything (everything) else. *Nothing* mattered...not anymore. But regardless, it was late summer. He knew this, because he was sweating in the lobby of one of the tallest buildings in St. Paul, Minnesota, as he watched the old-fashioned dial show the lone elevator descend from the eighteenth floor. His destination was the fifteenth. This would be his third--or fourth, he wasn't certain--visit.

Thorne had suggested that Randy see this new guy, this new "doctor," and he was certain it was because the therapist was tired of his cell phone going off at all hours. *Can I see you now? It's happening again! Can't you clear your schedule?* Randy was *certain* it was because of the *sights* the good Dr. Thorne wouldn't admit to having seen, having...*experienced* for himself first hand.

And that brought him to St. Paul and Dr. Michael Bailey, who had begun thinking that he'd write a fine paper on this case, perhaps find himself alongside that blowhard Richard King in *Therapy Breakthroughs Quarterly*.

That hope was cut short, because Randy Conroy, AKA Session Heading HN-913104, Session Recording A-D, brought something fierce and evil that last visit to the fifteenth floor.

Turned out it was the fourth session after all.

††††††

[Session recorder device is switched on.]
Excerpts, S4 Transcription--Dr. Michael Bailey, August 14, 2012. 5:45 PM.

"Good evening, Mr. Conroy." Bailey was not sweating, despite the heat. Foregoing an air conditioner, he compensated with a side window open by several inches.

"Hi," Conroy sat, almost jittery. "Thanks for seeing me on such short notice." He paused. "Again."

"Quite alright," Bailey had a deep voice, but also one of compassion. "You are officially my last client of the day. And as they say, no rest for the wicked. Besides, you seemed quite...agitated on your voice mail."

"Yes, sir, I--"

"Still thinking about Abigail?" Straight to the point.

"Always." Conroy had a fixed stare at a pencil holder on Bailey's desk.

"And you still intend to not make an attempt to call her?"

"It's almost been a year," Conroy was shivering, just by remembering. "I'm...I'm not free of this curse. She's safer this way. She's safer not seeing."

Hmmm, Bailey thought, *here was something new.* "Care to explain?" He took a fresh pencil from the holder, and moved his writing pad forward.

"Well," Conroy said, haltingly. "I'm, ah, seeing..."

Well, maybe not. Best to nudge him along. "Them again?"

"Yes, sir. Ever since--"

"The incident on the Queen Mary," Bailey interrupted him again.

"Yes, sir," Conroy didn't even notice, "ever since the Queen Mary."

"You know, Mr. Conroy," the doctor leaned back in his chair. "This is our fourth session and there has been no provocation in regard to these spirits or ghosts you speak of."

He then mentioned Thorne's name, but Conroy was lost in thought momentarily. *Abigail. Top hat. Supernatural Tour. Half-visible sailor. Abigail.*

"He was afraid," Randy finally said. He knew full well that Thorne had lied about why he had sent him away to a big city doctor.

"Of?"

"I think you know."

"But that's just the thing, Mr. Conroy," Bailey moved forward again, "I've seen your scars, I've heard your stories. Listened to you describe every little thing that happened to you. And I've collected the same specific moments recollected in your grandfather's files." He paused. "Yet I have never seen one single out of the ordinary moment in all of our sessions. Four sessions and the only clinical explanation I can give is--"

"The wiring in my head is all fucked up?" This time Conroy interrupted the doctor, and both shared a laugh.

"Well," Bailey smiled," I wouldn't have put it so...eloquently."

More laughter hissed onto the recording.

"Dr. Thorne said the same thing, at first."

"So," Bailey looked serious again, "may I ask what provoked your agitation enough to ask me to stay after hours?"

Complete silence, later written down as thirty-seven seconds.

"Mr. Conroy?"

"Sorry," Conroy's head jostled, "I just..."

"Is it the voices again?"

Another pause, fifteen seconds elapsed.

"Let the record be shown that patient 2013-119, Mr. Randy Conroy, nodded his response as an affirmative."

"Sorry." Conroy's head hung low.

"Not to worry. It happens. You say or do what feels natural. It's my job to keep track so that I can help you diagnose and--in all likelihood--cure you of your affliction."

Bailey cleared his throat, and continued. "So, where were we? The voices again, right?"

"Yes, the voices."

"And what did they have to say this time?" Back and forth again. Ping-Pong of the soulless, as they say.

"They..."

"Go on, son." Bailey motioned around him. "This is the safest environment imaginable. The voices said what exactly?

"They gave me a warning."

The hissing tape recorded the sounds of graphite on paper.

"Mmmm-hmmm," Bailey said. "And this warning was?"

Another pause.

"Remember, you're safe here. No harm whatsoever can come to you." Bailey made additional notes, then prompted Conroy again.

"The warning?"

"To stay away."

"Mmm," Bailey said. "Stay away from what?"

"From you."

There was the sound of the pencil dropping onto the paper, lightly rolling away from the sound of the recorder. There was a pause in the session that lasted a complete half-minute.

"Me?" Bailey's eyes widened.

"You." Conroy's voice was dull.

"And why do you think that is?"

"You know," Conroy had his hands on his knees, no longer looking at the pencil holder. "Life is supposed to be small. If you want something grand, *adventurous*, if you want true and everlasting love--"

He paused to laugh at that, and then continued.

"--a happy ending, well then, you go to the movies, you read a book. Life, *real* life, is supposed to be linear. Uneventful. Not this."

"And what do you think 'this' is?"

"You turn on some cable channel, any one, pick one, and there's all these episodes on UFO sightings, ghosts and Bigfoot, the Loch Ness and the Lake

Champlain Monsters. Mothmen and chupacabra. *All these stories*...and all these people telling those stories look like they forgot to pop their meds or were waiting for the next beer after the camera panned away." Conroy paused. "This isn't supposed to happen to ME. Not me. I'm not crazy, I didn't believe in these things, and now...now there is no escaping them."

"Things?" Bailey showed a bit of impatience.

"You always make me say it."

"It's my job, Mr. Conroy."

"*Things* as in ghosts," he sighed. "Ghosts aren't real, they are nothing but empty sheets. *They don't exist.*"

"Yet, you believe that some sort of *thing* warned you to stay away from me? So you believe *something* exists."

"I wake up screaming," Conroy had said it time and again, "the same time, every single night."

"What do you believe it is that's causing you to awaken in such a manner?" The pencil was back in Bailey's hand. "Dreams? Stress? What is so unusual about these nights?"

"I feel..." He paused. "I feel hands."

Another period of hissing silence from the recorder, longer than the rest, and then the voice of Dr. Bailey was heard.

"You know, I'm not at liberty to discuss my patients, past or present, and although your grandfather was not my patient, still, I *have* read his files in order to better help you and your case. So although I cannot go into detail, I could perhaps ask you if you were aware that your grandfather recounted similar feelings? Scratching noises,

208

reaching hands, strange voices. There must be some similarity, don't you think?"

"I do." Conroy answered simply, then went silent again.

"You know, Mr. Conroy, from what I've read here, you seemed to be more open with Dr. Thorne--make it noted that patient 2013-119--Mr. Randy Conroy, has shrugged his reply of--"

There were faint sounds that could be considered children's' laughter.

"--I was saying, I, um..."

"Dr. Bailey?" Conroy asked, his brow furrowing with concern.

"Yes, let's procee--"

A mind can do funny things, and something like a tape recorder would record what ends up being truthful. Conroy heard the rumbling of the office cleaners rolling giant garbage cans in the hallway. Bailey had heard an inhuman growl. And wanted more than anything else to leave.

"Right, then. Well, our time is up, unfortunately and--"

"But you said you would stay...Oh my God, you heard it, didn't you?"

"Heard what, I didn't--"

The children laughed again.

"As I said, Ran--ah, Mr. Conroy--the session is over. We can resume--"

And then the true mayhem began, everything from that point forward documented clearly by the St. Paul Police Department's Forensics Lab. A loud crash and a thump suggested the end table lamp closest to Bailey's patient had broken after hitting the carpet.

The session had started at a quarter to six that evening. Things spiraled out of control by 6:25 PM.

"It's not a figment of my fucking imagination!" Conroy was shouting now. "Now you see exactly what Thorne did! NOW YOU KNOW EXACTLY WHAT THORNE DOES! It followed me from the…"

"Randy," the doctor stuttered. "I think it best if you leave. We'll resume this--"

6:27:33 PM. The large oak-framed mirror exploded outward.

6:27:38 PM. For the next several seconds, soft popping sounds suggested the overhead tube lighting shattered in short intervals, as if something had been poking into the ceiling towards them.

6:28:01. A scream that seemed more like an echo, even the Night Watch Commander had trouble describing what he heard.

6:28:07. Bailey could be heard muttering "Jesus Christ!" several times.

6:28:10. A deafening crash.

6:28:14. Bailey again: "Oh, God. Help me, please--"

"He seemed to levitate out of his chair," Bailey spoke into the *new* recorder in the early hours of the morning, this time for the benefit of the police, as well as his own patient records. "The lamp and mirror broke, the ceiling lights shattered. He was spread out in the center of the room, mid-air, suspended upside-down as if in crucifixion. His mouth was open as if he was trying to scream, but I heard nothing. *His face was inhuman.* And then his skin just ripped open. It just...ripped away...And then I heard what sounded like--"

And at that point, Bailey's fragile hold on reality snapped. His head lolled down as the last syllable drooled from his mouth.

Several weeks later, results came in to the St. Paul Forensics Lab. The process had been sped up as best as humanly possible, normally a request to the decoders at Fort Meade, Maryland, would take months.

This is what the end of the report read:

Bailey's voice, slurring, then the thump of his face hitting the steel table.

[Analysts confirm third voice below frequency level Juliet Tango.]

[Analysts using {REDACTED} confirm presence of E.V.P. phenomenon.]

[Language has been confirmed by {REDACTED} as ancient Samarian.]

[Final notation: the word Dr. Michael Bailey had spoken has been definitively translated using {REDACTED} as the word:

††††††

...Mine....

CHAPTER FIFTY-FOUR

Flatline Echoes

The next several months, in ellipses...flatlines on a screen...random synapses trying to form a single coherent thought. Dot dot dot equals the drip drip of saline...drip drip drip equals the blood spatters during Randy Conroy's terrible, final visit with Dr. Michael Bailey.

Conroy had several surgeries after the events at the therapist's office, *extensive* surgeries, specialists coming in from California and New York to assist the Mayo Clinic in downstate Rochester.

He had almost died.

...flatlined...

Several times, his clawed skin sewn in patchwork fashion.

...flatlined...

Victor Frankenstein would be proud. He would *admire* this monster of flesh and stitch.

...flatlined...

New wounds, seemingly appearing overnight, the specialists never understanding, but finally their patient was stable.

They spoke of the procedures in a normal fashion, trying to forget their own personal glimpses into madness.

Touch and go, they'd say. Simple as that. And eventually Conroy healed.

At least his body did.

The last straw was mild, the one that forced his hand the same way it had his grandfather's.

He had been sleeping, badly, as best he could. Any rest, however brief, was a reprieve. Comforting to be back in his grandparents' home.

But the sheets would start to move of their own accord, the lamp nearest him would turn on or off at random intervals. Chaos, and then normalcy. And then the lamp would lift up and throw itself against the wall with such force that it exploded across the bookshelf and table, silver coming down like razor rain.

Conroy would awaken at such moments and an invisible force would backhand him across the face. And it wasn't too long after that final operation that his defeat had taken its toll.

After an attempted suicide in a filthy, rented apartment in downtown Minneapolis--layers in a damnable city, hell, why make his grandmother clean up the mess if she ever returned, when strangers would do--Conroy was confined to the same asylum his grandfather had been in. Committed too. *Black River*. The one where he had killed himself. The same one where he, unlike Randy, had succeeded in his escape.

The doctors talked amongst themselves about the odds that Conroy had survived that bullet from the WWII issued .45, how the bullet had curved around his skull, exiting without more than bruising brain matter, swelling which had gone down within days.

Randy Conroy, hotshot journalist. All gone. It was ALL gone. The tailored suits, the toned bodies at the fitness clubs and on the streets of his old

Manhattan neighborhood. His dreams of getting out, of treasure hunting and penning the stories and tales told of fiction, of rising higher than any other member of his godforsaken family, all gone and unraveled into the same madness that took his Papa.

Painting the walls with his own blood, his crimson life, as he rocked himself and drooled, telling tales, his blood as ink, tattered flesh as pen, of strange markings, of fantastical artwork, and of haunted worlds. Upon the walls, the floor, the ceiling of the padded cell, every space available. Modern ships turned ancient, shadowy forms seemingly worshipping a man in a top hat and grin.

The doctors stopped their visits, most days Conroy was silent. Others, he would tell of a pattern to another side, the "Other Side," another world of some sort, and that these stories he had written in red needed to be studied, accepted as truth. Learned from.

So that nobody else would fall into the same nightmarish world.

So that the hauntings would stop.

✝✝✝✝✝✝

October 13, 2014.
Two years.
Zero progress.
This is my life, Conroy thought, over and over, again and again. He lost count of the times. *A prison of bone and flesh.*

He stood naked on an unknown shore, his body covered in tar and filth. Before him was an endless river, its surface fire and lava. *Hell*. In the literal sense. Haunting, and deep inside, past the nightmares and shadows that lay all around, he felt the truest essence of pain and sorrow.

Looking down, he saw a broken and scarred frame. There were fresh lacerations crossing over old scars. There was a bloody stump where his left hand had been. His eyes were pale then, the colors of the river fading, and Conroy knew that his soul was starting to flicker and fade along with it.

Echoes and flatlines...

In the distance, he could suddenly make out the familiar form of the Queen Mary, pushing away the lava in its wake. Suddenly, burning bodies fell from above--*Heaven's light? Maritime Law of the dead?*-- and he was distracted by a doctor and a nurse standing on either side of him. They were clearer and more defined than the rest of the scenes of madness before him.

"Can you hear me, son?" A man's voice. A doctor with his pen light.

I am lost and left behind," Conroy continued in thought. *An echo, searching until the end of time.*

He then went back into the waters, lava burning his thighs.

"Randy?" That same male voice, reassuring to no avail. "I am a doctor, I can help you."

Conroy was wading waist deep through the waters then. Demonic vultures, carrying stillborn babies from their bellies, morphed into German soldiers as they landed gently on the deck of the Queen Mary.

Conroy continued walking.

"Randy, please tell me what you see..." This time, Conroy's mind wasn't even acknowledging the other voice in his head.

Though if he had, he would have answered thusly: A nightmare.

He screamed upon seeing Abigail's image in intense, undeniable pain. He looked on helplessly. His own back was cross-hatched with the scars of whips and claws. Her face, contorted by fear, then the terrible sound of her voice screaming.

She was bound to a pillar of meteorite souls, held tight by thorny vines that were eating into her flesh as black clouds formed overhead.

"Please, God, not her!" he screamed.

Mr. Thetepet was beside Randy now, the image of the doctor forgotten.

"The Lord?" Mr. Thetepet grinned wide, the lava reflected in his perfectly-sharpened teeth. "God does not remain here. *We do*."

"NOT HER!"

The doctor and nurse were standing in the padded room, Conroy strapped to a chair in front of them, screaming for Abigail's soul. The doctor turned toward the door, promising himself that he would save this man from whatever hell he was in, no matter what.

"Doctor?" the nurse asked.

"Watch him," he replied. "I need to make a phone call."

✝✝✝✝✝✝

Abigail Marshall looked like she was in a classic movie staple; a petite, once pretty little thing sandwiched between a woman and her child--the little kid wailing at octaves usually reserved for shattering glass or calling dogs--and a man whose own girth alone looked like it exceeded the maximum weight limit of all the other passengers on the 737 combined.

Her left shoulder was crushed under the weight of the sleeping man's overflowing triple chins and her right eardrum was stinging from the child's cries of discomfort.

Coach, it's the only *way to fly*, she thought ruefully.

But little did Abigail know that it *wasn't* the altitude. The child was crying having seen her face.

A monster on flight 815.

Oddly enough though, Abigail didn't seem to notice, she was able to tune the cramped confines into oblivion; because she was still thinking about a man a half a world away. She never really stopped thinking about him. About a love named Randy Conroy.

A ghost.

Chiseled good looks*, so truly handsome* she thought, seeing him so clearly in her mind's eye, as she closed her baby blues and fought for what little comfort remained. His face, that look, never fading, never giving in to the fogging haze of memory. Not yet at least. It was still love. And there would never be another.

The truth was, Abigail knew that his strength, his virtue, those piercing eyes had been reduced to nothing. Reduced to whatever the darkness, which held his sanity, wished. Nothing but dust and echoes remained.

Yes, she looked like the classic movie staple heroine, *but this wasn't a horror movie, like her life had become*, she thought with clarity. Not here where all these other lives remained ignorant to the true horrors which lurked close by, on the opposite side of reality, but real enough to appear in the blink of an eye. Real enough to destroy lives and claim damnable souls. She had seen it happen. She knew. Nothing would stop them if hunger willed it so. If the devil desired.

Only Abigail had already faced one nightmare. Wherever she went, whoever she met, they could see the result of that nightmare that had taken half of her face. They could see that she was still very much haunted.

Like Randy had said to her before he pushed her away, Abigail to be once again left alone with her thoughts, nothing would stop it. *Nothing will stop HIM.*

Mr. Thetepet. The Tempter.

Randy's voice still echoed in memory. Just as potent. Just as strong as the image of his face, of their nights making love when everything felt normal. *Safe.* When she had found the one she believed to be her soul mate. The one she wanted more than any other, the one she could not save. This wasn't what her life was meant to be.

No, no right now this wasn't the life she had always dreamed of and it certainly wasn't like a horror movie, not yet at least, not up there, 35,000 feet above. But it *was* her life. It was *all* her life.

She knew that fully, just as she knew that the real *horror* would come once the plane landed.

Yes, she thought. She knew this.

She had *always* known this.

And Abigail Marshall had a feeling that ghosts, were the least of her worries.

CHAPTER FIFTY-FIVE

Black River Mental Health Facility
Black River, Minnesota.

Dr. Anthony Midwell, the head of the Black River psychiatric ward, escorted Abigail Marshall down toward Randy Conroy's room, which was at the far end of the pristine corridor. They spoke in hushed whispers as they passed other doors, other corridors, other rooms of madness and incurable despair, the talk anything but cheerful and optimistic.

Listening to what the doctor had to say, Abigail was absolutely shocked (horrified) to find that nobody...*NObody*...had visited Randy, not family, nor friends, since he was committed. No one cared enough to even call...He was alone. Abandoned.

Randy Conroy WAS a ghost.

"Doctor, be honest," Abigail said, trying to keep the ruined half of her face turned away for the doctor's own benefit. She was certain he had seen enough troubling sights in his lifetime, she would spare him her own. "Will he recognize me?"

"I really can't say, Ms. Marshall." He looked defeated. "He spoke to one of the other doctors here, one who works the graveyard shift. I've memorized what your...well, I memorized what Mr. Conroy had told him, the notepad is still in my office drawer and, quite frankly, I'm afraid to even look at it anymore."

"What did he say?" Abigail looked equally defeated, but more than that, she looked...terrified. Abigail was visibly shaken. And rightly so.

The doctor's voice trembled and she noticed that his eyes wouldn't turn away from the door that they would both soon enter. He was a man who looked like he, himself, had seen the *things* connected to Randy Conroy's presence...he looked like a man haunted by such sights.

"Blood may still pump through my veins, my heart may still beat, but I have ghosted myself from all of your lives long ago, Mr. Conroy had said. *I was rude and insulting, disrespectful and vain...I was* hurtful *to* ALL *those I crossed paths with. I cared more about my vanity, my materialistic world, and the value of the paper in my wallet over what truly mattered. I lived each day as if I was* above *all others...and I* deserve *the devil because of it. Because I turned my back on my own blood and family, on all those who would care for me. Who would love...I am nothing now, nothing but the dust and echoes of life."*

Abigail wasn't just defeated, she wasn't just terrified. Abigail Marshall was heartbroken. Without the man that she loved, broken or not, she felt *lost*.

"Please understand that I've heard such stories in my profession, Ms. Marshall. *We all have*. But from *his* mouth, we have heard such *horrors*...I had left the boogieman back in my childhood closet where he belonged, but here, when in the same room with Mr. Conroy, it's like...not to be dramatic, but it's like the boogieman still exists. It is like he is watching us."

221

The two orderlies, who had followed behind at a polite distance, walked up to stand with the doctor as Abigail eventually entered the room. She immediately gasped and fought back tears at what she was witness to.

The handsome man with whom she had fallen in love with, the man who had *saved* her, was now reduced to a drooling, thin mess. His eyes were bloodshot, she imagined it was from a lack of sleep and bouts of crying, maybe rage. Her own mind, though she did not want to admit this to herself, seemed to crack a little bit more as she realized something disturbing.

The images, the forms, the shadowed figures and mindless creatures were no longer the story Randy's grandfather had illustrated with his own blood. No. It had become a *new* story.

Randy's story.

Their story.

She knew he was lost in the dark corridors of his mind, and she wondered if his staying in this room, one so similar to that of his grandfather's, was truly helping.

But she did know one thing. She was right, ghosts *were* the least of her worries.

"It must be fate," she said, her laugh was filled with sorrow, as she kneeled and then sat beside him. "Us sitting here."

Randy did not speak a word.

Abigail saw that his left hand moved, his fingers covered in charcoal and drawing a deep, black circle, an endless pit of darkness, again and again. They were the rings of Hell. The place he was lost...

"Randy? Baby?"

She could not look at the wall behind him, at the menacing gaze, produced in the form of Randy's own art, of the man in the top hat and grin. But then she smiled a small, hopeful smile.

"Maybe I could spend a little time with you."

His hand stopped moving. There was a small flicker of recognition in his weary eyes. She extended her hand out to him, like her smile, and her eyes, the flush of her skin, it was so inviting.

"For just a little while," Abigail said.

And then Randy smiled, faintly at first, as fresh tears fell, and he gently took her hand in his own.

"For just a little while."

Epilogue Note:

To this day, the legends and phenomena of the Queen Mary have been shrouded in mystery.

There have been no deaths of tourists in its history.

At least, none that were ever reported.

AUTHOR'S NOTE

I love the idea of the "adventure." I love it with all that I am. No matter if it is found within the pages of literature or within the celluloid of film, regardless of the genre; no matter it be my GREATEST passion and love that is horror (and ALL of its branches) or if it is found within the quest of science fiction. From romantic comedy to western, from the "Other Worldly" to the real world, from science to mysticism, no matter drama or the hard boiled and smoky haze that is noir...

Adventure rules my dreams.

Adventure is the reason (right behind my parents) why it is I "*chase the stars.*"

It is what I crave. And it is the principle reason why I am an author and an actor. You see...I am so very fortunate, so *very* lucky and blessed in my life and in my career. As an author and as an actor I have battled for the fate of worlds and I have seen the other sides of nightmare...I have been able to weave those stories and tales born of my imagination and dreams upon the written page and, in turn, I have known such dreams and I have lived such lives.

But every now and then, if we are lucky, we (our *true* selves, our *honest* selves) experience an adventure *beyond* our wildest dreams. Beyond our greatest imaginations...

If we are lucky, we experience an adventure that not only dares us to dream...but one that tests us. One that tests our hearts and strengths, our truths and beliefs...

As corny and dramatic as it may all sound, if we are lucky, we can experience an adventure that tests the very light of our souls. An adventure not being filmed nor written, one not being watched or read...but rather, one being "lived."

Lived by *us*.

And quite possibly, one that was always (and only ever) meant for us. One that was *born* FOR US.

Like I had written in the novel you now hold in your hands: "*Harker had his vampire. Holmes his Moriarty. Arthur the very blood and lineage in his veins. Victor Frankenstein his monster...Conroy had the devil.*"

In my humble opinion, those were moments, *adventures* that tested those heroes, those grand men...they were moments that will echo for an eternity because of it.

And no matter what ANYONE says...WE, you and I, can have those grand and epic adventures, as well. You and I can have the very stars.

And that is truth.

We just have to be unafraid to chase them.

Call it fate or destiny's design. Call it faith. Karma or happenstance. Call it what you will. At the end of the day, it marks you. It changes you.

Is it for better or is it for worse? I honestly don't know...that isn't for me to decide or say. To each his or her own. And to each, their own adventure lies ahead for them and them alone. Just as it does for you.

That is why I dream of telling (*being a part of*) stories that can not only remind people why it is they fell in love with the horror genre, but why they fell in love with stories and tales told in the first place. I dream of stories that *dare us to dream.* And, in turn, stories that make us fear the darkness once more. Those stories that get back to the true darkness and psychological side of the monsters that lurk not only within horror, but with US.

"*Whispers in the Cries*," the novel you hold within your hands this very moment *is* a work of fiction, yes.

But...

But there IS a truth to some of it.

Believe what you will and trust in that...listen to your heart and not your head, because that is what will guide you to the truth.

The only truth...

And this is mine.

I had experienced something while researching the history and location, the legends and lore of the grand vessel that is the Queen Mary. I had experienced something during my four nights aboard the Queen Mary that taught me about *true adventure.* It was that rare experience that took me into another world. An adventure that showed me a world unlike *any* I had ever before known.

Like Randy Conroy, (only for the briefest of moments) I saw the "Other Side."

I chased the stars...

And although the adventures--from finding Abigail and knowing the truest *gift* of her love, to the nightmare horrors of Mr. Thetepet and his demonic brethren--although they ARE FICTIONAL, born of this author's imagination...SOME of the things within the pages of this novel, in turn, hold *truth*.

This IS a work of fiction; let me say that once more. *This is a work of fiction* (obviously), but some of the places, some of the locations such as Mound, Minnesota (where I was born and raised) DO exist. While others are a product of my imagination, created in order to better help tell the tale I so greatly wanted to tell. Places like Bright Spell, Minnesota and the Black River Mental Health Facility...they do not exist on any map, and one could not find them even if he or she happened to wander off the beaten path of any road...they exist only within these pages. And maybe we're better for it...

But when you blur the lines between fiction and reality, you do your *very best*, with honor and respect, with appreciation, gratitude and awe, to capture the essence and grandeur of those places, of the "truths" and "facts," while also giving equal care to the *fiction*.

That is truth. The Queen Mary. Mound, Minnesota. The poem "*Love after Love*" by Derek Walcott found within the prologue...they exist within that truth. Although much more inviting, much more beautiful and warm.

But like I had said...there is also *another truth*. And that truth is whom I happened to cross paths with while onboard the Queen Mary. You can find my experience with that otherworldly wanderer in Chapter Nineteen. And you, on the next page or so, can see for yourself what "I" had captured within the viewfinder of my camera while exploring the Promenade Deck at The Devils Hour.

Whoever he was. WHATever he was...I cannot say. That knowledge, that truth is far beyond me. It isn't something for me to know. Not yet, at least...

But what I do know is this: it was an experience, an *adventure* that I will never forget.

And who knows...maybe for the one I've come to call "Old Salt," maybe it was an adventure for him, as well.

I only hope that there are many, *many* more to come.

And until they do, I will be here...waiting.

-- MATTHEW EWALD
FRIDAY, MAY 20, 2011

Old Salt

About the Author

Matthew Ewald has come from a number of movies ranging from theatrical releases to made-for-cable dramas and thrillers, as well as A.F.I. Independent Productions. He was fortunate enough to have portrayed Nicholas Bluetooth on the highly popular FOX science fiction / adventure television series "Galidor;" the "Galidor" franchise an international hit spawning Matthew his own action figure, as well as merchandising rights through Cap'N'Crunch cereal, McDonalds Happy Meal Toys, XBOX and Playstation video game consoles, among many others. He recently wrapped production on three films, was a part of an award winning web-series, as well as having the great honor to have filmed the serious-minded remake of the 1959 classic Edward D. Wood, Jr.'s magnum opus, "Plan 9 from Outer Space." Matthew is a member of the HWA, as well as a published author with numerous horror stories, and two horror novels already to his credit. With an impressive body of work and a slew of upcoming projects at the end of 2011 and well into the upcoming year, Matthew is looking to stake his name as an up-and-comer in the genres that he so greatly loves.

Wherewolf by Franchisca Weatherman. 978-0-9833773-7-5

When a pack of werewolves hits a small southern town, the local Sheriff realizes this is one case he can not solve alone. He calls in the F.B.I. to help him take down the killers that are taking the lives of the local teens. When the wolves abandon the town for the streets of New Orleans during Mardi-Gras celebrations, the hunters become the hunted in an all-out war where no one may survive....

Electric Angel by Sue Dent 978-0-9769947-9-4

Because of her cancer, Anna Chadwick wouldn't live long enough to carry her twin infants to term. Yet she wanted nothing more than for them to have a chance at living. Learning one would be stillborn didn't lessen her desire.

It would take a miracle....so she prayed for one.

When an electrical entity arrives to take the place of her stillborn, some would reflect that prayers aren't always answered the way we'd expect them to be.

Demon Revolver by Jason Gehlert 978-0-9822530-7-6

Jason Gehlert offers three terrifying tales of bone-crushing mayhem, blood soaked screams, and demons around every corner. In his first short story collection, Gehlert pulls no punches, delivering on a wide spectrum of genres. The horror western "Revolver," the gritty sequel "Woodsman 2," and the macabre fantasy tale, "Ghost Bride."

Fracture Time   by Alan Draven
978-0-976994787

Donovan Vicar is a "feeler," a man who feels the vibrations of people around him. He embarks on a late bus ride to seek out Timothy Crane, a man rumored to be dabbling in black magic, and finds himself in 1957 and a town plagued by missing young women.

Human Nature by Matthew Ewald   978-0-9842136-6-5

The only survivor of the grisly aftermath of an activist raid on an animal testing lab leaves him institutionalized. When his psychiatrist begins to unlock the secrets to the events of that fateful night, she finds it is up to the both of them to stop the unspeakable evil that was unleashed upon the world.

You're Dead Already....Living in Hell
by Jake Istre   978-0-557-01083-7   A Diverse Media book

Jake Istre--- Highly popular underground cult writer and bassist, actor and high-end restaurant chef who personally prepares meals for such celebrities as California Governor Schwarzenegger; author of such acclaimed works of poetry as "Shocking Tales of Murder & Insanity" and Sacramento's crowned resident "street poet." Presented here are intense, explicit, raw and highly personal collected prose and short stories mirroring a life's dark journey of experience, angst, love and loss, drugs and twisted death and sex and high times lived to the fullest. Do partake and enjoy. "One of the top 5 poets of 2005!" ---Preditors & Editors 2005 Readers Poll

The Everborn: Special Edition by Nicholas Grabowsky   978-0-9842136-0-3

The Everborn concerns the offspring of fallen angels that have lived among us since the dawn of man. Throughout the ages, they live life after life in normal society until each one falls in love and fathers their own child. Before that child is born, they undergo a rapid degeneration into a fetal state before they disappear entirely and become reborn into a new life. When an Everborn is reborn as a set of twins, one a soulless serial killer on a quest to be born again into a sinless life and the other a kind-hearted ghostwriter for a world-famous rock-and-roll horror novelist, a banished Watchmaid claims her role in an ancient prophecy to use the soulless twin as a means to re-enter our world and bring about its destruction.

Unholy Repression by Jessica Lynne Gardner 978-0-9833773-8-2

Cole Carney longs to find a way out and begin his career as a school teacher. After a strange incident, the mysterious Father Stanton gives him a job at his old elementary school but he soon finds that more than just the decor has changed.

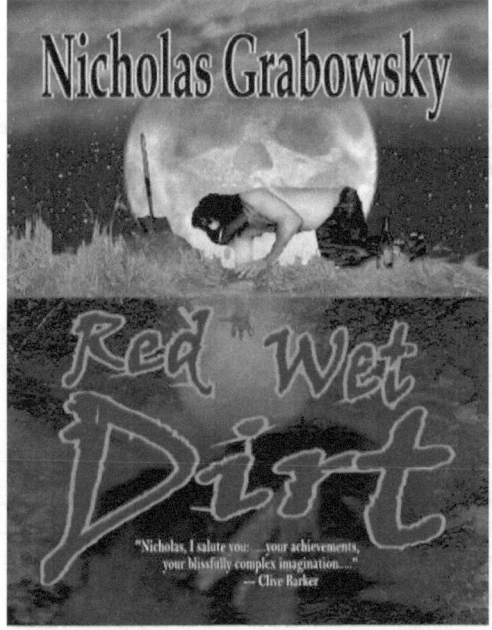

Decayed Etchings by Brandon Ford   978-0-9833773-9-9

In his first collection, Brandon Ford delivers 18 brand new, never before published tales of the dark, twisted, and macabre. Buried within these gnarled pages, you'll discover jilted lovers, cheating spouses, bizarre fetishes, acid trips, and roaming sleepwalkers. You'll meet noisy neighbors, struggling writers, vengeful females, and even a monster or two.

Chophouse by Horns   978-0-9842136-8-9

A sinister night falls over the relaxed rural community of Dominic County. Before the light of day would return to the quiet woodland town, many came to believe that the gates of Hell had broken open and the Devil's minions were rampantly spreading terror and death there. The Chophouse is OPEN!

Meat City & Other Stories by Jason M. Tucker
978-0-9842136-9-6

Take a trip along the arterial highway, and make a left at the last exit to enter Meat City, where all manner of nasty things are clamoring to greet you. Granger knows what it's like to kill a man. When the corpse of Granger's latest victim staggers to his feet though, all bets are off. These and other slices of horror await you on the raw and bloodied streets. Enjoy your visit . . . .

COMICS THAT DON'T SUCK.

Look for
us
wherever
books
are sold.